Inflicted

Explorative Tales of What
Breaks and Binds Us

Leo Otherland

Edited by Theodore Niretac Tinker

BALANCE OF SEVEN

Dallas

For information, contact:
Balance of Seven, www.balanceofseven.com
Publisher: dyfreeman@balanceofseven.com
Managing Editor: tntinker@balanceofseven.com

Interior and Cover Illustrations by Zu, Azuzel23
azuzel2369@gmail.com

Custom Font and Cover Design by Peyton Freeman
www.artstation.com/peytonfreeman

Line Editing and Formatting by Theodore Niretac Tinker, TNT Editing
www.theodorentinker.com/TNTEditing

Proofreading by Amanda Mills Woodlee

Japanese Language Consultant: Nyri A. Bakkalian, PhD

Publisher's Cataloging-in-Publication Data
Names: Otherland, Leo, 1989 - .
Title: Inflicted / Leo Otherland.
Description: Dallas, TX : Balance of Seven, 2022. | Contains 8 b&w
    illustrations.
Identifiers: LCCN 2022945806 | ISBN 9781947012301 (pbk.) | ISBN
    9781947012318 (ebook)
Subjects: LCSH: Emotions – Fiction. | Healing – Fiction. | Pain – Fiction. |
    Self-realization – Fiction. | BISAC: FICTION / Fantasy / Dark Fantasy.
    | FICTION / Psychological. | FICTION / Science Fiction / General.
Classification: LCC PS3615.T44 2022 (print) | PS3615.T44 (ebook) | DDC
    813 O85-- dc23
LC record available at https://lccn.loc.gov/2022945806

26 25 24 23 22   1 2 3 4 5

For the broken ones.
For those in the shadows
who are hurt by the light.
You are not alone.
You are far from alone.

Contents

Introduction

"You must think me stupid and childish when you've been through so much more than I have."

"Pain is pain. It all hurts the same."

Those lines come from what I consider to be the first truly successful fiction I ever wrote. Though I've grown as a writer since bleeding my heart into that first story, I still cry every time I read it. Because I didn't write with others in mind; I just wrote out all the pain that needed to be expressed.

While that might lead to extremely personal writing that you might question showing to others, the *response* to that intensely personal piece of writing, which I delivered to whatever passerby would have it, taught me otherwise. People read my bleeding words and said, "That's me. That's how I feel. Someone actually said how I feel!"

Alone with our pain, we are tempted to think that what we feel is stupid and childish and no one would understand. We might believe that if we ever met someone who *actually* had a reason to be in pain, they'd ridicule us for being petty. Yet when we dare to take a chance and show people the honest pain we carry, a few will see it and return, "I get it. It doesn't matter how our pain is different; it's still pain, and I get it."

"I get it" can feel like the most powerful words ever uttered at times like that. They can't take away the pain, but suddenly, you're no longer alone with it, and that can make a huge difference.

After discovering I was neither alone nor being petty, I decided that I would keep telling people they weren't alone either. So when I was approached with the possibility of writing a collection of short stories for Balance of Seven on a theme close to my heart, I chose the theme of brokenness and pain and the multiple ways we as people deal with them.

Inflicted is the result of that choice of theme. This book combines stories I had at least partly written before this project was ever an idea and others I wrote directly for this collection. But no matter how or when I first conceived these tales, they all speak to the same underlying theme: an understanding of pain and brokenness.

All books undergo evolution, shifting into new forms until finally attaining cohesion. *Inflicted* has been no different. I looked at the body of work I had generated and had to decide how, precisely, all the pieces fit together. I knew they did, but like with any puzzle, I needed to rearrange the pieces before I found their homes.

In the end, I realized the collection contains two sections, with one story balanced between them. One deals with the breaking process and the pain that causes it, while the other portrays already broken characters and how they choose to handle their pain and scars. Tying the two sections together is a story called, fittingly enough, "The Glue."

"The Glue" was written specifically for this book, and I knew from the beginning it needed to be special. It became the "intersection" of *Inflicted*, the place where characters both break and decide how they will deal with their pain.

On one side of "The Glue" are three tales in which people break: "Compulsion," "Requiem in the Wires," and "Empire of Clouds." On the other are two stories about already broken people: "Any Other Day" and "Kintsugi."

I started writing "Compulsion" before *Inflicted* was ever a dim inkling in my mind. It began with the prompt of "the darkness of humanity," but as I wrote the piece and later viewed it through the lens of this collection, I came to realize it was more about breaking than darkness. My character had done nothing but lie to himself for his entire life. His break became a release.

In a similar vein, "Requiem in the Wires" deals with the relief that can come from breaking apart. When I wrote this small, grim tale, I wasn't thinking about it being in this book. I was barely thinking at all. Mostly, I remember being in a dark place and needing to release part of that pain before I fell apart. "Requiem in the Wires" provided me the same relief my character found in ruin.

Born from the same initial prompt and a vastly different mindset, "Empire of Clouds" is about as far from "Requiem in the Wires" on the spectrum of breaking as I could get. Both may be about someone breaking, but the reasons involved are nothing alike. "Empire of Clouds" showcases our willingness to break when we believe the intended outcome is worthwhile.

On the side of people dealing with their brokenness and pain, both "Any Other Day" and "Kintsugi" were written with *Inflicted* as a whole in mind. And oddly, both were inspired by the work of a certain friend of mine.

Of the two, the idea for "Any Other Day" is definitely the older. I read a small, completely unrelated piece my friend had written, and a tiny grain of an idea got lodged in my head. It sat there for close to a year before *Inflicted* became a reality and I sat down to write. That little, undirected flicker of inspiration then bloomed into what has become my favorite piece of writing in this book: a snarky, morbidly humorous story about staying alive even when we're broken and don't want to.

Meanwhile, though inspired by the same friend's writing, "Kintsugi" is as different from "Any Other Day" as

Introduction

"Requiem in the Wires" is from "Empire of Clouds." This was the last piece I wrote for *Inflicted*, and it has always felt like the natural ending to the collection. "Kintsugi" is all about mending our broken pieces and the question of whether we deserve to.

No matter the story or its journey, all these pieces express the truth of pain and brokenness as I know it. Now, with the words on paper, my only hope for these pages is that someone will read them and at some point say, "That's me." Because if they do, they'll know they are not alone.

Compulsion

I dreamt, as always, of warmth and darkness. The dreams might have been comforting, like lying in the safety and security of my bed, but the warmth was too hot and the darkness too visceral. Together, they wrapped me in deadly serenity, permeating my being with pleasured leisure.

Yet the serenity itself was unsettling. Even as I reveled in the warmth and darkness, I knew I *should not*. The leisure inspired anxiety, and they wove together until they were inseparable. Desire and guilt each sharpening its claws on the other.

Coming awake to the vague memory of warmth pouring over my fingers was like waking from the vulgar dreams of prepubescent arousal. Yet I had not been young for a long time, and while my dark dreams were never more than pure sensation, I understood exactly what my traitorous mind wanted. My fingers itched for it—the embodiment of *should not*—but I had left it behind for something better. Something valuable and beautiful.

Beside me, Lynn breathed steadily. I turned my head to

watch the dim, early-morning light filter through the blinds and gild him in dusty luster. That unreliable light sketched him with softened lines and contours. Dusky shadows and the folds of the thin sheet pooling around us shrouded his lean, toned form, converting his hardness to muted angles. Lying on his stomach, his arms outstretched to grasp his pillow, and his rust-colored hair tumbling about his relaxed face, my partner hardly resembled the man he was while awake.

I thought he was the most beautiful at moments like this: unconscious and unassuming.

Trusting.

Anything could have happened while Lynn slept beside me. Absolutely anything. Yet he lay there at ease.

The shifting light of the twin suns' first rays glinted off a band encircling Lynn's finger, and the sight tugged dully at parts of me still buried in anxiety from the dream. The ring had adorned Lynn's hand for over a year now. A matching gold circle twisted around my own finger like a brand.

Partners.

More.

Lynn had never been one to observe the etiquette and niceties society demanded for a life to be "right." It was one of the things I liked about him. When he had asked me if I wanted the ring and I had accepted, we simply signed a few papers and said a few words at the courthouse.

It had been the first and last time I ever entered a place of law and civil justice. Sometimes, I thought Lynn must have noticed my discomfort, but he never said anything.

So I wore the ring. It was what I wanted. It proclaimed that I had managed to do something right and worthwhile. It was the reason Lynn lay there so unconcerned.

He was beautiful, and he was mine. I had won him over.

A thin smile overtook my face, pulling to one side in a parody of playful mirth. Lifting a hand that still felt coated in thick, sticky heat, I gently touched Lynn's bare skin.

We were both bare under the sheets, but the helplessness of Lynn unclothed beneath my careful, caressing fingers inspired more than just base sensuality. What stirred within me was as arousing and terribly anxious as my quasi-formed dreams. I barely touched him, lightly dragging fingertips and blunt nails over his exposed skin, but there were so many other things I *could* do. Things Lynn would have been unconscious of until too late.

I bit my lip until it bled. Not much, just a single pearl of hot liquid welling up under my persistent canine, but it tasted like bitter lust. My fingers twitched roughly against Lynn's skin, and I quickly withdrew my hand, but the damage was done. With a deep, drowsy sigh, Lynn opened his eyes.

In that instant, the sleeping Lynn I admired transformed into the waking Lynn who constrained me. The seductively pliant beauty of soft angles and muted splendor altered completely with only a blink and a husky grunt, becoming the man I felt compelled to please.

I, too, underwent my own transition. The caricature of mirth disfiguring my features melted into something mellower. I licked away the blood clinging to the edge of my lip, and a softer smile pulled my whole mouth into a melancholy curve that bore no resemblance to what it replaced.

I often wondered if Lynn ever caught me in such moments. Perhaps he had noticed something not quite right in my expressions or mannerisms. But if he had ever seen anything he did not understand or felt uneasy about, he had never shown it.

Just as he now showed no sign of following the changes in my face as he woke.

Perhaps we were both liars.

"Good morning," I greeted, my voice giving away nothing of such thoughts.

"Hey, beautiful," Lynn rumbled, voice thick and sleep roughened. He swallowed and inhaled deeply as he shifted on the bed and ran a hand down his face. "What time is it?"

"Early," I admitted. "I did not mean to wake you."

A humming growl sounded in Lynn's throat as he rolled onto his side and reached for me. He brushed long strands of hair from my face, tucking them tenderly behind my ear before rubbing the pad of his thumb over my lips. "I never mind being woken by you, lovely."

Lovely. Beautiful. Lynn was always using some epithet in place of my name. The rare times *Alise* came tripping off his lips always caught me off guard. My name seemed foreign coming from his mouth, so I never knew what to do when he spoke it aloud.

I was glad he did not speak it now, in this morning moment of half-light and groggy waking. If he had, I would not have been able to hold my gentle smile. My lips would have trembled with the desire to form something more unpleasant, and he would have felt that twitching under his thumb.

"I know," I murmured into the pad of his thumb. Slowly, I reached up and touched the hand Lynn held against my face. I laid my palm against his skin, slipped it over his wrist, and traced my fingertips down his arm.

That gentle caress was all it took. Lynn seldom needed much invitation, and the combination of morning arousal and wordless bidding was enough for him to cup the back of my head in his hand and draw me in. Our lips met, and Lynn's fingers burrowed into my inky hair as our legs tangled together.

From there, it was all hungry gyrations and greedy hands on soft flesh. Sleepy, pleasured leisure engulfed us—different from what I found in my dreams but no less full of heat. We contented ourselves with hands and mouths and nothing else in the gilded morning light. We had done more the night before, when I had taken everything Lynn would give me in hopes it would drive the guilty desire from my mind and the anxious itch from my fingers.

He had been unable to sate the desire that haunted me then, and he was no more able in the cool light of dawn. I smiled at him and cooed pleasantries of fulfillment once we had finished, but when I rose from our bed and turned away, the hollowness of perverse need still snaked through my limbs. I bit my lip again, seeking the salty taste of blood.

I had to hide the desire when Lynn came up behind me, placed his hands on my hips, and kissed the shell of my ear. "You want to take a shower, babe?"

He meant together, I knew. I agreed, like the dutiful man I was, the ring on my finger a heavy reminder.

When we were through, I was at last left in peace. Lynn knew I often withdrew into myself, requiring space and time before I could respond smoothly again. I frequently wondered what he thought of that, but I never asked and he never said. So many things were simply left unspoken between us.

Once, Lynn would have tried to draw me out of my isolation, luring me with patience and kindness, but he had abandoned that approach in tiny increments. He still left me openings, of course, and sought me out during my silences and thoughtful absences, but it was not the same. Where he once would have stalked me openly, he now trod warily, uncertain whether he hunted prey or another predator who could strike back with tooth and claw.

I flicked the comparison away like dust from clothes that had hung too long in the closet and began to dress. Lynn had adjusted, that was all. Relationships were fluid, ever changing. To expect otherwise was foolish. Even I had changed in trying to give Lynn everything he wanted. In trying to *be* everything he wanted.

That was what one did for a partner, was it not? That was the way of the right and orderly world. When one found a worthwhile mate, one did everything possible to please them and keep them.

Or was I wrong in that assumption?

The eyes that stared back at me from the floor-length mirror burned. Dark and bottomless, they were eyes to get lost in. The day we met, Lynn told me that anything lost in my eyes would be irretrievable. It had been a strange compliment, edged with an unease that did not quite reach the brink of concern. A fine line separated fascination and fear, but Lynn had yet to cross it, then or since.

That thought I smoothed away with a pass of my hand down the front of my button-down shirt. I was meticulous about what I wore, which provided a safe place for my attention. The quality of the deep-blue silk of my shirt was a far safer consideration than the substance of my dreams, the knowledge my partner held of me, or what I did not know.

There was no reason for me to dress so carefully. I would not be leaving the house or allowing anyone but Lynn to see me. But dressing myself with care and detail was something I did for myself and no one else. It was a simple thing, an unnecessary gesture, but it belonged to me as few things did.

I passed my hand over my shirt one more time and checked every line of my pressed black pants before padding away from the mirror and back to the bed.

The place where Lynn and I slept was as rumpled and soiled as we had left it. Dispassionately, I bent and stripped the bed bare. Being with someone could be as dirty as other, less acceptable desires, and I had no wish to sleep on soiled sheets that night. Instead, I disposed of them in the hamper before painstakingly remaking the bed with fresh linens. My talented hands moved without conscious command, taming unsightly creases and smoothing unruly wrinkles.

When I was through, the bed was pristine, waiting anew for Lynn and me to disturb it. Satisfied, I left the bedroom, descended the stairs, and allowed myself to think on other matters of the day.

As always, my attention turned first to the kitchen. Lynn required a healthy meal to start the day, and I would not allow him to go without. He might have been capable of preparing such food for himself, but I seldom permitted him to do so. He might insist, but such instances were few and far between. He seemed to understand how affected I was by his doing something I considered *my* responsibility. My duty as a good mate.

Lynn provided for us. He should not have to think about household matters as well.

I paused in the kitchen doorway and surveyed the faux marble and shining chrome. Last night's dishes were washed and neatly arranged in the drying rack, and what I needed for this morning was set out in orderly rows, ready for use. It would be a simple matter to fulfill this ritual task.

Padding quietly into the room, I glided my fingers over the objects I had laid out. I lingered over the knives, fascinated, but a sickening resurgence of the guilt from my dream cut my admiration short. Turning away sharply, I left the knives for the moment and narrowed my focus to the individual tasks, the better to ignore the itch in my fingers.

Setting the bamboo tray on the counter, I focused on it as I filled it: A dish of fresh fruit I cut with practiced skill went in one corner. Another of yogurt offset the first. A plate of eggs edged with toast cut into triangles settled in the center. A portion of oatmeal garnished with berries joined the plate. And a mug of coffee with only the slightest addition of whole cream finished it off.

The consuming work comforted me. I lost myself in the rhythmic complexity of the individual preparations and the timing required for all the pieces to be completed at the same time. The intricacies cooled the itch in my fingers and mind.

Such distractions never lasted long enough. The activities I used to keep my thoughts from my own needs always came to an end, even as my needs remained unattended.

If my fingers twitched or my canine dug into the corner of my lip as I brought the tray to Lynn, he either did not notice or chose not to comment. Instead, he broke into a smile and wrapped his arm around my hips to bring me close to his side.

"Thanks, beautiful," he murmured against my waist. "I don't know how you make everything look like this every day. It makes me feel special."

"It is meant to." I allowed him a few more moments of holding me before I slowly eased away, disentangling from his clinging grasp.

"Aren't you eating?" he asked as I moved off. "You skipped breakfast yesterday too."

"I eat during the day."

The words were a simple excuse for a fundamental difficulty. During meals together, Lynn always wished to be near me and just *talk*, as though there were more to discuss than the repetitiveness of each day. It wore on me, and I struggled just to reserve mental energy for the final meal of the day.

"It is more important that you eat. There is no guarantee how your day will play out. You might not eat again until you come home."

I could feel his eyes on me as I turned away. It stung him, I knew, but even as I attempted to be all he wanted, I failed in several respects. The inadequacy plagued me as persistently as the itch in my fingers I could not soothe.

That he could not fulfill my own needs was beside the point. I *should* have been able to give him what he needed.

The reminder of my failures made me sullen and withdrawn as I cleaned up the kitchen. My thoughts distant, I plunged my hands into the warmth of the fresh dishwater and idly curled my fingers around something sharp. The sensuality of the liquid heat engulfing my hands tugged at something primal within me, calling to mind the hot, viscous unreality of my dreams. Swirling my hand through the water, I watched the undulating whirls that followed my movements, mesmerized.

Suddenly, arms framed my body, and hands slid over my wrists. "Babe, you're bleeding."

"What?"

Even as the word slipped from my mouth, I noticed the pinkening of the water. Lifting my hands, I watched shining beads of blood well along two fingers of one hand.

"I must have cut myself on the knife," I said absently as my thumb smeared the blood across the cut fingers. The sight of red streaking my skin sent little tremors throughout my body, and the corner of my mouth hitched up in an unpleasant smile that I quickly tried to smooth out.

It was a compulsion, this itch in my fingers. They sought to *do*, even when my mind instructed them to *do otherwise*. The realization nearly pulled a tearfully hysterical burst of laughter from me. Biting my lip, I managed to hold it back to a whimpering hiccup and blink away the water in my eyes.

"It's all right, sweetness," Lynn rumbled into my ear, his face resting in my hair. "They're just little cuts. Let me put bandages on them?"

"All right," I agreed through the tightness in my throat, even as the salty taste of my blood grounded me.

Lynn pressed a kiss to the shell of my ear and moved us, joined as we were, to a stool at the kitchen island. He settled me there with a cloth to sop up the blood. I sat like a child, transfixed by the red welling through the white cloth, until Lynn returned and hunkered down in front of me.

He slowly wrapped his larger hands around mine and cradled them. "Are you doing okay, babe?"

"Yes," I answered faintly. I felt like I was waking from another dream and Lynn was the unreality in the room. It took a series of shallow breaths for me to focus enough to smile at Lynn and tenderly brush my uninjured hand through his hair. "Thank you for taking care of me."

"It's my job, babe." He carefully unwrapped the small bandages and curled them around the middle phalanges of my first and second fingers.

They were silly things, the bandages. Bright and color-ful, they were designed for children. When Lynn bought them, he had simply taken them off the shelf without look-ing at them beyond making sure they were functional. That was Lynn: utterly unconcerned with the niceties of society. If his job had not had an enforced dress code, I doubted he would even know what clothes to wear.

It was endearing. Perhaps it struck a chord of paternal instinct buried deep within me, the part of me that wanted something to care for. It was probably the reason I insisted on doing all the things I believed Lynn should not.

Too soon, the moment passed, just another distraction. It was little more than a wisp in the day.

Lynn told me to just leave the dishes or put them in the dishwasher for once. Kissing each bandaged digit, he pulled me to my feet so he could take my hips and dance us slowly across the floor by way of goodbye. "I'll be back, beautiful," he said. "I love you."

"I love you," I returned, and perhaps it was not a total lie. Surely some part of me felt for Lynn, harboring attachment and affection. Whether that amounted to what people called love, I did not know.

Was not love giving yourself to another?

Or was I wrong in that assumption as well?

Thinking such things did little to still the obscene need building in my chest or ease the itch working through my fingers, so I did not dwell on them. Turning from the empty doorway through which Lynn had left, I did as he had instructed and filled the little-used dishwasher. It likely needed to be used simply to ensure it remained in working order.

Another failure on my part.

Once the dishwasher was running, I glided into the living area and surveyed the space. Pristine wood furnishings sided plush couches. Surfaces glowed, and pillows were artfully arranged to give the too-clean space a lived-in appearance. There was nothing for me to do here, and hardly more required my attention on the second floor.

Lynn kept his own office—the single room I did not touch—and I had not claimed any space as my own. The closest was perhaps the closet where I hung my array of clothing. For the most part, I tidied what was not mine and prepared meals I rarely ate.

There was little in the house to hold my attention, and within the silence, I could almost hear the ticking of some immense clock counting down the hours of my life. The walls enclosed me, stark and hard. I could have left at any time, yet I seldom did.

Things happened when I did, things I could not take back. Instead, I told myself it was better to wait for Lynn each day. I strove to live a worthwhile life, and I could not if I indulged myself too much.

Absently, I pulled a book from a shelf and tried to lose myself within its pages. However, the words were familiar, and all I managed to lose was the trail of the story. Far too soon, the book dangled from my fingers as I stared wistfully at the wall. Dull images I could not name flickered through my mind like afterimages of my dream.

That was how the first text of the day found me: *Hey, babe. How's your day?*

It was Lynn, of course. I knew it before I even consciously registered the phone in my hand and the words displayed in their small text bubble. I knew it even though his number was not saved in my phone. Lynn was the only person I spoke to, the only person with contact information for me.

I sat with the small rectangle of a phone cupped in one hand and the forgotten book in the other and contemplated the oh-so-easy replies my fingertips usually tapped out: The casual reassurances Lynn required throughout the course of my never-changing days. The knowledge that I was here, that I was secure, that I loved him, and that I would be waiting on his return as a proper man should.

As a decent partner would.

The book thudded to the floor from numb fingers, and a mirthless smile quirked the side of my mouth, even as the hand holding my phone shook. I was such a failure of a mate. I had tried, but ultimately, I was a failure.

I stood and ran a hand down my shirt to smooth away imagined wrinkles. I supposed I had known from the beginning that I would be, but I had given it every piece of me I could.

Need, however, was a powerful thing. One could only deny it for so long before losing oneself to it.

I could deny mine no longer, just as I could not bring myself to skim my fingers over the screen of my phone and fill a responding text bubble with placid untruths.

Part of me noted that the book lay page down on the floor, its pages bent at awkward angles, but I left it where it had fallen. From a drawer of the nightstand by the bed, I collected my wallet and some money. They were the only things I took whenever I left the house, aside from the phone in my hip pocket. There were keys on the coffee table and a sleek car in the garage, but neither was mine.

Under the cool, bronze light of the twin suns, my feet carried me to a lounge and bar I knew in an upscale portion of the city. The suns poured hued light through the thick windows, painting everything in a haze. I sat in the mellow streams and watched little text bubbles appear unanswered on my phone's screen.

I love you, beautiful. I hope you're having a good day.
You've been quiet. Are you doing okay, sweetheart?
You there, lovely?

The messages popped into being under my fingertips, and I caressed the edges of the phone after each occurrence without responding. An untouched drink stood by my hand, and an amused smile decorated my face. Across from me sat a younger man, eagerness in his every gesture. I thought he must be in his twenties, and though I was not so young anymore, I still had a few charms. Lynn certainly seemed to enjoy me and had no misgivings about indulging in me.

Guilt accompanied the thought. I should not have been there—*should not* have done so many things. But guilt could no longer restrain me. I had embraced it and moved past it.

My inviting smile never wavered as I stroked the other man's hand with my fingers and watched his cheeks go pink. He was young enough and primed with just enough alcohol to be reckless. To fall in lust with the dark-haired man in the deep-blue silk shirt who gave him attention and possessed dark eyes he could get lost in.

The first time I had done this, I took my unfortunate admirer to a convenient hotel and paid for our room in cash, with a little extra to ensure the attendant forgot he had seen us and made the registration paperwork go away. Assuming we were there to do something lewd and unseemly, he had agreed, and he had no doubt regretted it when housekeeping had gone to clean the room in the morning.

I did not care about the location, though. Elegant hotel rooms, the back seats of cars, against alleyway walls. In the end, it amounted to the same thing: the taste of blood in my mouth and warmth flooding over my hands.

The only thing I ever concerned myself with was the man who had never found me. The papers had said a "Detective Decain" was the one responsible for the investigation of so much blood in the streets, but either by design or by chance, he had never come close to understanding me. Sometimes, I thought he imagined I had gone away, buried under the trappings of an ordinary life that claimed us all and left us caged.

Many times, it felt like this was only between the two of us: Decain trying to fix it all while I held on to loose ends that could not be tied.

The blood could not be put back, after all. I had tried, yet here I was, smiling amusedly at the warm body across from me and wondering where I would take him. What location would satisfy the itch crawling inside me.

Most places I could take him would make this easy, but the idea of easy made my lips twitch into something neither pleasant nor alluring, but bordering on the frightful and macabre. An imitation of mirth, it set off the tiniest of alarms in the man sharing my table. Uncertainty flashed across his face, but it did not linger as my features smoothed out.

I trailed my hand over his and up his arm, leaning forward until my lips were just shy of his ear. "Do you want to come home with me?"

His shiver was answer enough as I climbed to my feet and extended a hand to him.

The choice of location was foolish. It was so very stupid, yet I did not care. The stark walls of the house I shared with Lynn felt burdensome even at this distance, and the faintest of thrills ran through me at the thought of defacing all that whiteness I kept so clean.

My dreams hung heavy around me, need accompanied by the feeling that I *should not*. But should-dos had flown away, and the younger man had a car. He let me drive, and I let him try to distract me with his hands between my legs. I had had so much practice being unaffected, though, he was pouting by the time I stopped the car in the driveway.

I took his face between my palms. "I will show you a few things if you come inside." He flushed at the promise. I could feel his heart pounding too fast, and mine sped to match it beat for beat.

It was a compulsion, this itch for something more. It was the indescribable understanding that everything in life fell short of meeting *need*. So we distracted ourselves, pretended all was well, and carried on seeking right and worthwhile lives. Yet in our hearts, we could not lie.

We grew tired of lying.

And eventually, we stopped.

Honesty, in the end, was not always freeing. Honesty could kill what the lie kept alive. Yet sometimes that death was better than continuing a life wrapped in disillusionment and pretty make-believe.

Maybe that was why I brought my catch home with me this time. For honesty's sake.

"You live here?" Awe permeated my prey's voice as we entered the kitchen, and I wondered absently if he had even told me his name. Not that it would make a difference.

I slid my arms around his waist from behind and swayed him back and forth. "We all make convenient prisons for ourselves."

As if in confirmation, the screen of my phone lit up. I held it loosely in the hand that still sported colorful, childish bandages coiled around two fingers. We could both see the latest text bubble: *You're worrying me, babe.*

"What?" Confusion and guilt marred my unnamed prize's pink face, but I stilled both emotions with a simple caress. He swallowed. "I mean, do you want to show me the bedroom?"

"I would like to show you something else." I nudged my hips into him, and he whimpered and stumbled forward.

It was so easy to maneuver him, it almost felt like a game. And the flutter of his heart at his throat assured me he liked his view of the kitchen.

"In here?" I nearly laughed at the sinful innocence of his scandalized tone.

"My favorite room," I purred. I set my hips against the rim of the sink and my phone on the counter. With my hands free, I turned him to face me with his wide doe eyes.

"Why's that?"

My lips quirked in an unpleasant smile, and I stretched like a cat. My garishly bandaged hand dipped into the sink behind me. "Because it holds so many interesting things."

My prey stepped back, confusion clouding his hitherto-aroused gaze. The movement was just enough to save him from a slit throat as the knife I pulled from the sink slashed across his collarbone.

It really did not do to put knives in the dishwasher. It was best to leave them in plain sight, where they could be reached without unwanted injury.

And with speed.

Pity I had missed with the first strike, though. Blood was flowing, but it was not enough.

"Come along, pretty one," I cooed, moving forward. "We were going to enjoy ourselves."

He gave a strangled cry and fled. He was off balance, though, and this was my territory. I had prowled within these walls until I knew every stretch of space. Calmly, I caught up with him and sank the knife into his side just as he reached the doorway to the living room.

With a cry, he clutched at his side and collapsed. Babbling unintelligibly, he clawed at the rug he had fallen across in an attempt to drag himself away from me. Expressionless, I stepped forward, grabbed him by the hair, and did what I had failed to do with the first swing: cut his throat open.

The body jerked and spasmed, then went still, red spreading out in a wide fan across the plush rug I had done so much to keep clean. I bit my lip and choked on a sob that was half laugh. There would be no cleaning it now.

No putting the blood back.

No taking it off my hands either. They were gloved in crimson. At least that was honest.

Both the knife and my cell phone were in my blood-smeared hands when Lynn came home. I had picked the device back up once the warm body I had brought home with me had gone cold. There had not been much to do at that point except watch my lover's messages appear with increasing frequency and urgency. The last bubble to pop up had only said, *For love of the gods, Alise, answer me,* which made me wonder just how often Lynn had worried about what I did while he was gone.

But then . . .

"You always have been a smart man, Lynn Decain." I lifted my gaze to his. He stood stock still in the doorway, his suit disheveled enough to reveal the service weapon at his hip.

"Alise." His gaze trailed over everything again and again, snapping back to me—casually balanced on the arm of the couch with my ankles crossed—after each revolution. As if I could make what he was seeing untrue.

As if I would.

"You must have known," I stated. "Yet here we are."

"It didn't have to be this way, babe."

His voice held a plea, but my lips quirked up in the smile I had worked so hard to hide from him. "But it is this way. Shall we?"

I unfolded from my repose and paced forward. The phone I let drop, the screen cracking over the final text bubble displaying Lynn's compelling desperation.

The knife, I kept.

Requiem in the Wires

At first, I wondered if he was drawn to me because I was lonely. I had never been off world before, and the strangeness of life aboard a ship—the silence of space, the feeling of simply drifting, the endlessness of it all—disturbed me. That I knew no one on board only added to my uneasiness. All I wanted was comfort—something to ground me, to give me a point of gravitational reference in the hollowness of space.

As much as it terrified me, comfort was what he gave me.

I was crying in my bunk the first time he came to me. After months in space, the loss of everything I'd left behind weighed on me, and I had hardly slept in days—weeks—I couldn't tell anymore. The crew cabin was nothing more than a large dormitory in the belly of the ship—"belowdecks," as the old space dogs said. It was filled floor to ceiling with bunks stacked one atop the other, but the closeness only increased my loneliness. In the dark, I listened to the murmur of voices—friends and acquaintances talking through the artificial night—but I had no one.

The humming began within the wall near my head. It sounded like the thrumming drone of the thin synth wires running behind the panels, but . . . more. It rose and fell in a rhythm the synth wires should never have been able to produce: a melancholy tune, the melodic strains of a lullaby.

It entranced me and pulled me out of my quiet tears. Caught in that humming melody, I fell into sleep without knowing it, and I did not wake until a crewmate roughly roused me to tell me I would be late for my rotation in the engine heart.

After, I heard the humming everywhere I went. When I was alone in the veins of the ship, the wistful song would come to me from faraway wires. In the engine heart, the bio-plasma injectors would thrum with music under my hands. As I walked the ventricles from room to room, the tune would echo to me like a voice I couldn't quite hear but knew was there. Sometimes, I could almost place what the voice was saying, but each time, the words would vanish like a shadow fading in the light.

At first, I dismissed it as synth feedback. Everyone knew the old bioships were a bit strange, with residual memory loops caught in their organic plasma. The old space dogs said the wires remembered what people forgot. Sometimes, they just played it back in vibrating loops.

But I couldn't pretend to hear feedback forever.

It wasn't long before I realized none of my crewmates could hear the humming. Whenever I asked someone if they could tell where it was coming from, they would laugh and pass it off as the landlubber being tricked by phantom noise. Or worse, they would look at me stonily as they told me to mind my own business and not go chasing ghosts.

I didn't understand, and the uncertainty weighed on me as heavily as the dark recollection of harsh words and harsher hands that had chased me into the vast silence of space. When I could no longer bear it, I gathered my courage and crept up to the mess table where the oldest space dogs sat during meals, quietly asking if I could join them. The men were weathered and hardened, and some had not set foot on a planet in more years than I had lived. However, something—perhaps my hollow eyes or the trepidation I could not hide—made them take pity on me. They allowed me to huddle among them and listen to their stories of the ships in deep space, where men could go years at a time without seeing a planet.

Once my heart had stopped pounding hard enough to burst, I haltingly asked about the humming in the wires that only I seemed able to hear.

The men grew quiet, their faces filling with some emotion I didn't understand.

After a moment, one of them disturbed the hush that had fallen, slapping me on the back. "You're just hearing the ghost. Pay him no mind, and he'll let you be."

I felt the blood leave my face, and my fingers went numb as they gripped the table tightly. "Ghost?"

"Aye," another growled, "everyone knows the *Oleander* is haunted."

"How?" I whispered. It wasn't the question I wanted to ask, but I didn't know the right one. I had no words for the curl of apprehension knotting my abdomen.

The men glanced at each other, silently exchanging messages I couldn't decipher. When they seemed to come to a decision, they began unspooling the story for me.

"It started when the *Oleander* was already old—at this point, these bioships are antiques, you know. Somewhere around her seven or eight hundredth voyage—who can really say—they brought on a new engineer to work in the engine heart and the veins. One of the ones people say are a little psychic—the ones who can just touch the synth wires and know where the *Oleander* is ailing. Bioships are more than half-alive, and this engineer could hear her and fix what no one else could find.

"Or that's how people tell it. However it was, he was a bit odd. He kept to himself, which isn't the best thing for a young spacer to do. It takes time for a man to settle in to the quiet of space. Until he does, the emptiness of it fucks with his head.

"This young one never had the chance to settle, though. First run, the *Oleander* hit a cosmic storm halfway to the Henge System. Things got shaken up; some wires blew in one of the major arteries. The kid went in to fix them so they could get the *Oleander* out of the storm . . ."

"Things went bad," a new voice said, picking up the story. Its owner stabbed at his food, his jaw locked. "The ship—she hit some rough patches. Sparks flew. Somehow, the engineer was able to soothe the wires, get the *Oleander* moving again. But he didn't come out of the artery. By the time they went in after him . . ."

The man shook his head and looked away, leaving it to me to finish.

"He was fused with the wires."

"You know how it is with these bioships," said one space dog in a voice like gravel. "They ingest organic matter to keep the bioplasma charged. They *eat*. They're *alive*. Sometimes, when they're hurt, things happen. There are reasons ships like this aren't commissioned anymore.

"By the time they got to the engineer, it was hard to tell where he ended and the wires began. They cut out as much of him as they could, but they couldn't get all of him. Eventually . . . what was left was absorbed into the *Oleander.*"

"He never left, though," said the man who'd begun the tale. "When he was alive, he would sing in the veins and the arteries. Now, some people hear him humming in the wires."

"He was from Vega," another offered, waving his hand dismissively. "Everyone from Vega sings."

"Just pay him no mind and keep about your own business," the first finished. "He'll leave you alone."

I swallowed and looked down at the table I gripped, my knuckles white and creaking. "What was his name?"

Again, the old space dogs conversed silently.

"Owen," one offered reluctantly or, perhaps, regretfully. "His name was Owen."

That night, I lay curled in my bunk, my face tacky with dried tears and my mouth filled with blood from the lip I'd bitten trying not to scream. The humming came from within the wall, and I could almost see the singer—the young engineer from Vega on his first voyage.

In my mind's eye, he was so much like me: Alone. Adrift in deep space. A boy who could understand a ship that was quasi-alive in a way no one else could.

I didn't believe in psychics or ghosts or the dead becoming attached to the places where they'd died. I didn't believe, but . . .

"Owen?" I whispered, voice tight and heavy from crying. "Owen? Is that you?"

My fingers stretched out and brushed over the wall panel covering the synth wires. I imagined I could almost feel the thrumming reverberations of the melody under the pads of their tips.

I spoke his name again, and the tone altered and pitched lower into a new tune.

Sickness climbed into my empty stomach. "You don't want to hurt me, do you? You've never done anything to hurt me. That isn't what you want.

"Is it?"

He gave me no answer beyond the humming, and nothing I did would dissuade him from his unknown intentions. His song didn't stop. It followed me from my bed to the engine heart—to every part of the ship I tried to escape to. I found myself speaking the ghost's name softly, trying not to be heard.

That was a useless venture.

Nothing remained secret for long on a ship where the crew was all anyone had, isolated by the immensity of space. People started avoiding me, only speaking to me to assign me duties. I became more alone than ever on the *Oleander*, and fear gnawed at me constantly like a worm burrowing through my system. It seemed I had traded one misery for another in joining the *Oleander*'s crew. In running away from what haunted me on my homeworld, I had run straight into . . . something else. Something I couldn't define.

I did not know which was worse.

The doubts and uncertainty culminated one duty rotation when I was sent to search out and repair a blockage in the synth wires. Alone in one of the veins with the echoes of my breathing loud in my ears, I tried to steady my hands so I could locate what was distressing the wires. But I couldn't calm the beat of my heart or keep from continually glancing behind me for someone who wasn't there.

I couldn't shake the phantom impression of heavy hands on my shoulders, and it compounded the fear that had been creeping over me since the humming began. Though I tried to continue my work, I soon dropped to the metal decking, hugged my knees to my chest, and rocked back and forth, crying into the rough fabric of my pants. It would have been a strange comfort for my tears to soak into the material, but the protective layer repelled moisture, and the bitter, salty drops only coated my lips and hands.

"I can't do this. I can't do this."

We were months from any planet, though. I had no choice but to endure until we reached the next system.

The humming I had come to know so well began in a section of exposed wires across from me, and I moaned something like a scream into my knees. Then I took a ragged breath and scrambled onto my hands and knees, pressing my wet face closer to the synth wires, whose cylinders glowed blue white with the bioplasma circulating through them. This close to the engine heart, the wires ranged from the width of my fingers to the circumference of my arms. The melody reverberated from them all.

"Owen?" My teeth caught my lip and worried it. "I wish you could tell me if it were really you. You are Owen, aren't you? I'm . . . I'm Ren. Maybe we can be friends?"

No response came from the wires, though the song they sang shifted.

I scrubbed at my face. Then I reached for the resequencer at my belt with one hand and pulled the glove off the other with my teeth. I did not believe in ghosts or psychics, but I could sometimes feel where a problem was in the synth wires by touch. Blocked or injured wires ran warmer than they should, as if running a fever. Just by paying attention, I could find damage with my bare hands.

"Owen?" I played my fingers over the wires, and the hum moved up the digits into my hands. "You are there, aren't you? I need help. I need . . ." What I needed was so much more than I could express, so I kept my request simple. "I need to . . . to find where the wires are blocked. Can you help me, Owen? I know you're there."

Beneath my fingers, the wires sang pleasure and shimmered through several shades—powder blue, cerulean, cobalt blue, indigo—indicating chemical changes in the plasma. I followed the kaleidoscopic smears with the tips of my fingers to a wire that ran fever warm and pulsed the faded purple of orchids that had once grown on my homeworld. Heart rate kicking up, I ran the edge of the resequencer over the inflamed wire and watched the orchid shade dissolve under the tool's laser light.

The ghost in the wires had shown me the way.

In the following days, he continued to do so. Abandoned by my crewmates, I stopped just saying Owen's name and began talking to him. At night, I would hum or sing along with him until I fell asleep, my hand pressed to the wall panel by my bed. During the day, I whispered to him and asked him to show me where the *Oleander* hurt or ached. I spent as many hours as I could hiding away in the bioship's veins and arteries, soothing her pains.

Only a few of the old space dogs still spoke with me. Some would sidle up to the mess table where I sat alone and ask if I was well. They would comment on the dark circles growing like bruises under my eyes or the loose hang of my clothing on my shrinking frame.

"You haven't been touching the synth wires, have you?" they asked more than once.

I would always answer no. Of course I hadn't. Everyone knew not to touch synth wires without protective gloves. The residual bioplasma was dangerous. It was the first thing engineers learned about bioships.

I knew that but paid it no mind. Instead, I talked with my ghost, the one only I could hear. His voice seemed to grow stronger as the days passed, but that could just have been my loneliness expanding as I lost all sense of time.

If I could now hear words in his song—clear words that did not vanish like phantoms when I tried to understand them—what did it matter? Everything—everything—was a dream in eternal space, threaded through with the humming song in the wires. The lullaby sang me down into dreamless sleep, even when I was awake.

It might have been months or years or decades after I first heard Owen's song that the *Oleander* hit the cosmic storm; I don't remember anymore. What I remember most are the sparks and the bioplasma spilling beneath my feet from ruptured injectors in the engine heart. I recall them with perfect, precise clarity. The rocking of the ship and the chaos it brought stole my breath, and my heart throbbed when the head engineer ordered us all into the arteries to patch up blown wires.

Owen hummed from every dangling wire, his song loud in my head, and I could feel that the *Oleander* was dead in space. I had been aboard long enough by then to feel the hollow stillness in every surface around me and in the tingling fibers of my own body.

"Owen!" I called, stumbling with every ripple of the ship as it was tossed by the storm. "Owen, I need your help! I need—I need to know how to get the ship moving. Please, Owen!"

The humming, which had long ago burrowed into my mind, purred louder. Cerulean, mauve, indigo, and amethyst sparked and flashed through wires that dripped warm bioplasma onto my face, pointing the way. I followed the path they showed me, until I was thrown off my feet and into a slithering coil of wires that spilled out of the side of the artery.

My head rang. Beneath me, red blood mixed with the orchid and cobalt of the bioplasma on the metal walkway, and I realized I had somehow skinned the palms of my hands, though I couldn't feel it. I couldn't focus on what should have caused me pain, though. Through the gap in the artery's side, I had spotted the wire that thrummed the loudest, buried behind interwoven capillaries and sputtering neurocircuits. Pulsing violet, it hung limply beside the interface it was meant to feed.

By the size, I knew it was a main; it was much larger and thicker than those behind the wall panel beside my bed or even those in the veins. If I could just get that wire fused to the interface again, I was sure the *Oleander* would be able to escape the storm that battered us.

Without a thought, I crawled forward, smearing my blood over the mass of tangled, injured wires that kept the *Oleander* alive.

The tight press of the wires and circuitry within the artery wall made my heart pound and my breathing uneven. My head felt light and empty. When something pierced my hand, I could only look down numbly. Heat that should have burned flooded the appendage, but all I felt was warmth. I watched blankly as a wire squirmed into my hand, stretching the skin.

The sensation of the wire burrowing into my flesh was both painless and disgusting. Sickness rose in my throat to blend with my lightheadedness, and I dropped onto my belly in the narrow space, blues and purples dancing before my eyes.

Humming wires surrounded me, swaying and murmuring. Their weight fell silently upon my back, tightening around me like a noose as the wires sought exposed skin. I jerked when the severed ends found tender places and plunged into me with aching precision.

I should have screamed—perhaps I even wanted to—but all I was capable of were quiet tears. My head buzzed, and my voice panted out in little whimpers, pleading and sad.

"Owen."

I restlessly moved my still-free hand across the metal floor, my fingers trembling as they inched me closer to the violet that called to me.

"I need . . . need to . . . fix the severed main. If I don't . . . don't . . ."

I coughed up bioplasma and stilled, drifting in a hazy non-dream.

"If I don't . . . the *Oleander* will die. We'll die. Owen. Owen . . . please . . ."

Blue-white bioplasma flooded what remained of my vision, and I could taste the milky chalk of it on my tongue and in the back of my throat. There was a wire in my cheek, one twisting in my stomach, and another piercing the base of my spine.

I felt it all, but none of it hurt. The humming filled and soothed me. The light in the broken main pulsed, beckoning me, and somehow my hand found its way to the bleeding end of the wire. Slowly, in a daze, I lifted the wire to the wounded interface. The inanimate conduit came alive in my grasp, contorting and squirming into the neurocircuitry it had been severed from.

Within the wires, I felt the *Oleander* shudder back into motion as the plasma flow to the ship's core was restored.

The storm continued to shake the bioship, but she began edging out of it.

In the blue-white light filling the artery wall, other wires coiled up my legs. One nudged at my mouth, seeking admittance. As my lips parted, my eyes fluttered, lulled shut by the melody that was now part of me.

At first, I had wondered if Owen was drawn to me because I was lonely.

Now that I am part of him—part of the *Oleander*—I know he came to me because *he* was lonely. Because he wanted someone to be with him. To be like him.

I know this. I know the truth.

Just as everyone knows the *Oleander* is haunted.

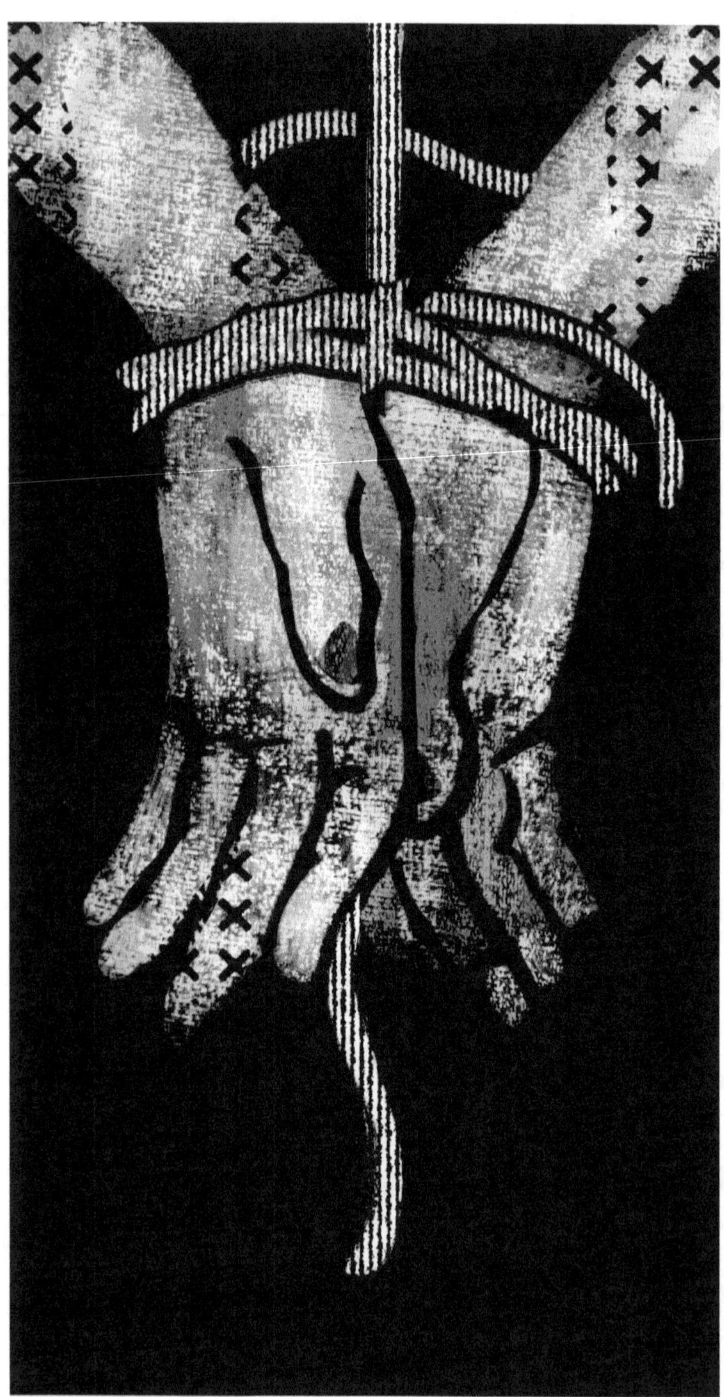

Empire of Clouds

Velvety darkness enveloped me. Stone and steel lay smooth beneath my hands, so cleverly worked, I could hardly discern where one ended and the other began.

My people were so very skilled in shaping hard, unyielding things to their will. With ingenuity and unflagging, unconquerable desire, they had even reshaped the world and defied what were once considered the laws of nature.

The human will was never to be taken lightly.

Not even mine.

In the dark, I brushed my hands over the joined stone and metal enclosing me. Through the walls and floor of my cell, I could feel the faint, ever-present thrum of engines churning in the depths. They never rested, those masses of gears and pistons and pipes, feeding on steam generated so far from this place that my people often forgot the steamworks existed.

"I do not forget," I murmured, tracing the ripple of vibrations in the stone.

The minute tremors were soundless. My voice was my

only companion in the dark, but I did not mind. I lay my head on the floor and slept, knowing my wait would not be much longer. The vibrations played through my bones, and my dreams were a riot of color, starting with black and ending with flashes of white, green, and bronze in an endless sky of blue.

The flashes were still bursting within my mind when a heavy, metallic clang jerked me from my rest and light like knives reflecting the sun pierced my closed lids. I put up a hand to shield my eyes from the assault, but my wrist was seized in a merciless grasp as the tread of many booted feet surrounded me. Twisting my arm and forcing me down, they maneuvered me onto my stomach.

"Asleep, my prince?" The affable, lilting voice came from some ways away, most likely outside my cell. Tadashi was not one to dirty himself, the arrogance of nobility a clinging raiment even his military appointment had not been able to strip.

Blessedly, he did not want an answer to his question, because I could not have given him one. The royal guard under his command held me down as one pulled my wrists to the small of my back and tied them there with soft leather. It was not meant to be painful, but my skin was bruised from previous bindings and each caress of leather along my skin rubbed it newly raw. I would bleed in time, but not now. Not even when the guards applied pressure to bring me to my feet, pulling the leather tight, did I bleed.

I did not protest the treatment either. I had earned this and would make no outcry against submission. Not aloud, nor even in the privacy of my own mind, though my body was another matter. I was cold, much of me ached, and I shivered as I was shuffled out of the dark space in which I had been held.

A laugh and a motion from Tadashi stopped me before him. "Cold, my prince?" His high, ringing voice called for attention, even as it cast shadows over me. He wanted an answer this time.

"Yes, Captain Tadashi." It was only natural. Everything but the thin under-kimono and riding trousers I wore had been taken from me. The cloth might have been long and flowing, but it did not keep me warm.

"A shame. I am sure you are unused to it."

My disheveled hair was fastened only loosely at the nape of my neck, and thick strands of it hung in my face, making Tadashi hard to see. Harder still when one of the guards nudged me in the back and I tripped forward, nearly falling.

I did not need to see Tadashi, though. Hardly older than I, he was the same as he had been before I left my home a fugitive. He was the same as he had been when he forced me to my knees amid the bodies of my loyalists on the surface, where the citizenry struggled simply to live.

Now, Tadashi was the only man present with silver staining the pristine black of his military kimono and chrome sparking at his wrists and earlobes. He was the only man with a gun tucked into the thick folds of the sash encircling his waist. All were signs of his rank and status among the royal guard.

"I am used to it, Captain Tadashi," I said softly.

"What?" rang my warden's voice. "Speak so as to be heard, my *prince!*"

The emphasis he placed on the title was poison, but I drank it down willingly, repeating myself with more volume. "I am used to the cold, Captain Tadashi. I was often cold among the common people on the surface. They do not see the sun, and the cold there holds one close—a counterpoint to the heat of the Dark Below."

Tadashi laughed. "How amusing. He speaks at last, even as we escort him to the Hall of Ancestors for judgment! Tell me more of your time on the surface, my prince. It amuses me so thoroughly."

The tread of my soft-soled shoes over the worn stone of the hallway slowed as sickness constricted my stomach. However, another nudge from a guard kept me stumbling forward and words tumbling from my lips. "I find nothing on the surface amusing, Captain Tadashi."

"Oh? Is that so?" Disinterest shaded his words.

I dropped my gaze to the progress of my feet across the thrumming floor, my mind full of churning engines fed by steam and the foundry where that steam was distilled from endless exertion.

"Tell me," I choked out through a tight throat, "have you ever been to the Dark Below, Captain Tadashi? Have you ever breathed the stifling air of that iron-and-steel hell, where the citizenry toil until their very bodies are used to fuel the steamworks?"

"What?" he inquired carelessly. "Lower myself to ob-serving the labor like a common guardsman? The very no-tion is unbecoming for one of noble birth."

"Then I have been most unbecoming," I whispered to myself. In my mind's eye, I saw again the black in which my dreams began. Since walking through the steamworks, I had been unable to banish that inky darkness from my con-sciousness. It seemed to coil up my body from the vibrations teasing at the soles of my shoes.

"*Unbecoming* is too gracious a word for what you have become, my prince." Tadashi's voice no longer held levity or disinterest. A small sound of pain escaped me, and I tucked my chin against my chest so he would not see the wetness starting in my eyes.

I had no right to tears. This was my own doing. I had begun it, and now I had to see it through to the end. No matter what bitterness came of it or how much it broke me.

The blood I had shed before leaving my home demanded it.

No more words passed between us as we walked. The royal guards kept close around me, using force to move me if I slowed or stilled or stumbled. I took it all without complaint and kept my head down.

It would not have mattered anyway if I had looked up. I could not focus on the world beyond the royal guard. Everything was compressed down to this tiny moment and the blood that filled my mind. It was only right I be punished for my crime.

Abruptly, the hallway opened around us and metal appeared beneath my feet. The hollow enclosure echoed with our footfalls, and I trembled as I realized what would come next. I tried to brace myself, but the suddenness of our dizzying ascension took me from my feet.

I found myself on stinging knees in the center of the cavernous lift, my body bent forward and my face pressed to the metal floor as I simply breathed. My head spun, unused to the upward rush after so long away from my home. I was struck and commanded to stand, but I could neither get my feet under me nor make my body move. At last, Tadashi instructed one guard to help me find my feet.

Swaying and sick, I expected a hard grip and rough hands. Instead, the arms that wrapped around my shoulders and waist were gentle, accompanied by soothing words in my ear. "I have you, my prince." There was no mockery in the voice.

"What is your name?" I whispered reflexively to the man offering me his strength to rise.

"Megumi, my prince."

"Am I your prince, Megumi?"

It was a fair question. Better to know than to deal with everyone indiscriminately. But as I regained my feet, there was no time for him to reply without being overheard. Besides, it was a question he could only answer through action, so I let it be and concentrated on remaining upright.

The steam-powered platform we stood on traversed the megastructure from its lowest hall to its highest peak, where the royal residence stood. I paid no mind to the dark chute through which we passed, however, as our momentum continued to dizzy me. I could only stand and breathe, focusing on my balance and trying not to sway into the guards surrounding me.

My inattention did not last for long, though.

Between one moment and the next, the stone was gone, ripped away, and glass and shining chrome took its place. I gasped and squinted, wishing I could shield my eyes as my vision whited out to nothing but *light* filled with flashes of green, bronze, and radiant blue—the colors that always concluded my dreams.

Guilt and awe blended in my heart once I could see again. We were climbing at remarkable speed through a cylinder of glass. On one side, dark stone rushed past in a blur; on the other was just space. Blue sky and white clouds hung in all directions, littered with darting shapes and the far larger, nearly still jewels that made up the floating isles of my home.

"The chancellor brought the whole fleet out for your trial, my prince," Tadashi informed me, his voice high and light once more.

I made no response this time. Instead, I let my eyes focus on the darting, glinting shapes: airships with glowing hulls and sails full of steam. They were beautiful, but they were nothing compared to the floating isles they flitted between.

This was the Divine Heights. Nothing surpassed the pieces of land my people had raised from the surface using steam and, most of all, desire.

Blue, white, green, bronze—the colors splayed across my vision in sharp contrast to the black in my memory of the Dark Below. Pained, I could not restrain tears this time.

Elder spirits, hear my plea.

The words tumbled through my mind, an incantation to summon the ancestors that I had been taught as I took my first steps. I pushed them aside as our upward momentum slowed and the platform reached the top of the cylinder. For what I had done, I had no right to appeal to those who had come before me. None.

Yet still . . .

Forgive me.

Before I could completely rid myself of the notion of forgiveness that I would not receive, the royal guard propelled me forward, off the lift and into the small courtyard of the royal residence. The urge to breathe in deep assaulted me as, for the first time in a long while, clean, open air surrounded me.

The desire had barely registered before more walls enclosed me. I was marched through more echoing corridors than I could have followed if I had not known them all as well as the patterns on my palms.

When I had left this place, I had known this would be my homecoming, but the knowledge made the experience no easier to bear. Pain worse than the ache in my arms and wrists and the hollowness of my stomach condensed behind my ribs. The mist of tears hindered my view of what passed.

It did not matter. The engraved doors of the Hall of Ancestors rose in our path all too quickly, obscuring everything else. My heart beat a quick dance, but I kept my head lowered as the doors were opened and Tadashi led us in.

As always, the hall was a strange mixture of dull contours and rich colors. The bronze walls of the cavernous space absorbed the light coming through the windows rimming their upper edges, staining the air muted hues and leaving the floor and corners in dim shadows. Within the shadows to either side of me, cloudy glass tablets marched along the walls in tiers that ascended from the open floor to the high ceiling. Each tablet was inscribed with the name and deeds of one who had gone before.

The far end of the hall was taken up by a raised dais, the foot of which was our destination. There, I would be judged by the chancellor and his council, their expressions stern and backs straight, the epitome of nobility upon their kneeling pillows. I knew this, though their forms were indistinguishable at this distance.

Before Tadashi could have me dragged there, a secretary in gray stopped him and spoke to him in low tones. When the secretary turned to retreat to the dais, Tadashi tittered at me. "You receive an honor, my prince. The chancellor wishes to have a private word before your trial begins."

There was an expectant lilt to his words, but I did not give him the response he desired. There was none for me to give.

My heart pounded as I scanned the shadows around and behind the thick glass slabs of the ancestor tablets. Hidden in the shadows and difficult to make out were others of the royal guard, guards who did not fall under Tadashi's command. My heart slowed at the sight, only to ache with guilt.

The chancellor's soft steps pulled me from fading

thoughts of my dreams and the colors that permeated them. "My prince," he intoned, and I raised my eyes to meet his.

Only to receive a slap across the face that had me stumbling back into Megumi's arms, the heat of blood rolling slowly down my chin from the corner of my mouth.

I stared through a tangle of hair at the chancellor—no, Harunobu. The strike had been meant to hurt, a personal attack. The title my father had given Harunobu had been left behind on the dais.

"Know this, my prince: but for my responsibility to tradition and duty, I would take your life into my own hands."

"I understand, Lord Harunobu," I returned, choking on the taste of my own blood, salty and hideous.

A flash of anger crossed Harunobu's features, and the blow of his hand rocked my head back a second time. If Megumi had not been holding me up, I would have fallen. Unwanted tears clouded my vision.

I half expected a third blow, but Tadashi's hand on Harunobu's wrist restrained him. "May I remind my lord that this man *will* die? Perhaps it would be best to allow justice the course dictated by tradition."

Ripping his hand from Tadashi's grip as if either the captain or his admonishment had offended him, Harunobu turned away and left us standing there. As he slowly returned to his place on the dais, my body trembled with the aftereffects of being struck and anticipation for what would come next. Once Harunobu had settled again upon his pillow, all my waiting would come to an end. As much as I had thought otherwise, I knew I was not ready.

"Prince Sada." Chancellor Harunobu's voice filled the hall, somber and dark. "You are called here to answer for crimes against your people, this council, and your very blood. Come forward to face your judgment!"

The royal guard shoved me forward. I nearly fell again, but many hands kept me upright until we reached the foot of the dais, where a small cushion sat reserved for the accused. I was forced down onto it gracelessly and without care. Fresh pain stung my knees despite the padding and cut up my arms as the leather bindings pulled tight around the chapped and delicate flesh of my wrists, but I made no sound. Tadashi and the royal guard under his command flanked me, a solid wall at my back.

"Prince Sada," Chancellor Harunobu repeated. Struggling to ensure my face did not reflect everything I felt, I lifted my gaze from the stone-and-metal floor beneath my knees. "What say you to this tribunal?"

"I am at your mercy, Lord Chancellor," I answered, my voice husky and rough with disuse and emotion. "Do what you have brought me here to do."

As the words fell from my lips, heat and agony exploded within my chest. I slumped forward over my knees, clenching my teeth and breathing heavily in an attempt to hold back the anguish that threatened to overtake me. I had no right to such grief, not when I had chosen to shed blood and to do so brutally.

But emotions could not be controlled by either logic or base will, and a wail of mourning burst from my throat, ringing through the otherwise silent hall.

The emotional purge lasted no longer than a single beat of my heart. By the time Tadashi's hand fell on my shoulder and pulled me upright, I had regained my silence.

"I would not have you miss what comes next, my prince," he muttered in my ear before resuming his position at my back.

I did not answer, and I showed no more feeling. I had

expelled my allotted pain; now I would face the consequences of what I had done.

One ancestor tablet stood out of place in all the ordered hall. Situated near the edge of the dais, it bore a fresh, deeply cut inscription upon its face.

Souto, it read. *King.*

There were other epitaphs engraved there, but I could not bring myself to read them. Instead, I focused on the device just visible behind the thick, translucent glass. I could not make out its shape through the glass, but it curved above the ancestor tablet's upper edge in impossibly intricate hoops and whorls of interlacing, etched metal. It gave the impression of a candle flame frozen in place, the source of the name my people had given it.

The lantern of the dead.

At a wave of Chancellor Harunobu's hand, the secretary in gray approached the lantern, a tiny golden ball cradled in one hand. The orb's minute size, however, was as deceptive as the lantern's stillness and inanimate appearance. When I was young, I was told such rare baubles contained enough compressed steam to fuel one of the floating isles for just shy of a year. I had even been given one to play with, an amusing trinket to roll about my room, as though hundreds or more had not toiled and died to create it.

Yet the orb the secretary held was no toy, nor was it destined to keep one of the jewels of the Divine Heights riding among the clouds. In this instance, what was most often used to fuel the lives of the living was presented as an offering to one of the dead, that he might see the light of the lantern and return for a short while.

My hands began to shake, hard enough to finally break the tender skin under the leather of my bindings. My wrists bled at last as a man dressed in gray placed a small golden ball into a notch in the lantern of the dead.

Yet the slow, hot slide of blood over and between my fingers was a distant feeling as the lantern's hoops and loops began to move. Slowly at first, they revolved in and out and around one another in a choreographed dance too complex to understand, even before their gyrations became too quick to distinguish. Then, all that remained was the illusion of a candle flame flickering behind the ancestor tablet.

In the faint but building glow of that man-made flame, the engraved glass began to burn, taking on a light of its own. Against that light, the fresh etchings blazed. The brightness pierced my eyes, and I wanted nothing more than to turn away or bow my head to avoid the fiery radiance, but I knew I would not be allowed to even if I tried. Tadashi or one of his guards would only force me back into my position of abasement.

Already, I could almost feel Tadashi's hand in my hair, forcing me to look. To watch.

And that would be right. That would be just. If I were to look away—if I were to try to avoid this pain—it would only be fitting for me to be dragged back to view it.

So I did not move, and I did not shut my eyes—not until the light became unbearable, flashing like electricity through the sky on a stormy night. Then, with a cry, I turned my face away perforce.

I trembled as the brilliance faded and the hall fell into muted silence. Slow tears trickled down my cheeks, turning my surroundings to golden-hued crystal. I did not want those tears to cloud my vision, but I could not stop them from flowing as I had before. The sight of the figure now standing on the dais, towering over me, had cracked my restraint.

"Father." The word fell broken and rough from my lips.

A blow across my back knocked me forward over my knees. "You have lost the right to address King Souto so, my *prince!*" Tadashi tittered from behind me. "Surely here, before the council, you will show greater respect for what you have done!"

Hampered by physical pain, I slowly straightened and faced the transparent figure standing before the ancestor tablet that honored his name and memory. My father's form was hollow, lacking solidity. Its edges wavered and flowed in currents unseen and unfelt by the living. Yet by design and base human desire, he stood there, called back from the realms of death through the light of the lantern of the dead.

My mouth felt dry as the ash and dust of the Dark Below, and guilt weighed heavy in my chest. But there would be no mercy for me. Nor should there.

"Prince Sada." Chancellor Harunobu's voice rolled out for the third time, his words claiming the attention of even the sorrowful-eyed spirit. "This day, we call forth your father to witness against you and pass judgment according to the testimony here given. What say you?"

"Speak the crimes of which I am accused, Lord Chancellor."

My ritual response was hardly more than a murmur in the large room, but it did not need to be. All those gathered knew what words I would speak, and my father's chancellor barely waited for me to finish before he carried on.

"Treason against this council; incitation of rebellion; conspiracy to ally yourself with our rivals to the north and their prince, Jouichirou; the betrayal of your people, whom you, as liege, should have protected; and the murder of your father and king. What say you?"

A numbness I could not explain burdened my lips as I

answered, and my words came out strained and low, almost heavy. "That I am guilty of all these crimes save one. I never betrayed my people. All I have done, I have done *for* my people."

Chancellor Harunobu's features darkened, his brows drawing down in anger. "For the good of your people, you murdered their king? For the good of your people, you aligned with a foreign prince who would take away their way of life and—"

"Is it for the good of the people that over half of them toil endlessly in a world without light? Is it for the good of the people that such unfortunates live and die in the steamworks so we few can ride among the clouds, forgetting by what power we keep our glittering isles afloat? Is this for the good of the people, Lord Harunobu?"

Layered with desperation, my voice rang clear for the first time since I entered the hall, loud enough, surely, to carry beyond the ranks of ancestor tablets to those who stood hidden in the dim shadows. I willed my judges to understand what I had witnessed, but I knew they would not. I could see it in Harunobu's face and feel it in the strike of Tadashi's hand against my cheek.

"You would speak so to the chancellor?" Tadashi demanded. "Truly, your arrogance knows no bounds, my prince!"

The imprint of Tadashi's hand upon my cheek burned and flared with pain, and I fell silent, lowering my head abjectly. This was my due, and there was nothing for me but to let it carry through to the end. I would receive my punishment for all I had done; that I had done it for the well-being of others mattered not. I had brought this upon myself.

"My king," Chancellor Harunobu called, returning to tradition. Reluctantly, I peered up through my hair to see him bowing respectfully toward the wavering figure hovering over me on the dais, before he straightened once more. "What testimony do you bring against this one, who is responsible for your death and so much suffering and unrest among your people?"

For his part, my father did not look at the man he had named chancellor as Harunobu invited him to speak. His deep gaze was reserved solely for me and my disheveled form. Though I lowered my eyes again to hide behind the curtain of my hair, I could feel his eyes upon me, lingering on the marks of mistreatment printed on my face.

"He speaks the truth . . . as it is in his heart."

Always—always—one expected the voices of the dead called forth by the lantern to be distant, but it was never so. My father's voice was light but sturdy and as sure as it ever had been in life. And in the wake of his words, my shoulders bowed beneath a mixture of grief and guilt, even as murmurs chased through the hall like ripples on a pond.

Glancing up, I saw Chancellor Harunobu's expression darken again. Whatever he might have said next, though, was lost amid a deep groan of twisting metal and shifting stone and the startled cries that followed. A deep, resounding alarm reverberated through the walls from a room deeper within the royal residence, a pulsing counterpoint to the stuttering of the reverberations emanating from the engines churning below.

For the first time since they had begun to turn, the great engines were hesitating.

The Hall of Ancestors—perhaps even the whole of the floating isle—shuddered. Startled cries turned to screams of fear as the alarm continued beating and the floor began to tilt. The cushion on which I knelt slid across polished steel and stone. Though I tried to brace myself by spreading my knees, I was thrown to the floor alongside several of Tadashi's royal guard.

"What is the meaning of this?"

Chancellor Harunobu's demand was quickly lost in the rampant terror overtaking the hall and the crash of an explosion hitting the isle, which canted further. Ancestor tablets tipped over, shattering upon the floor, and out from among them sprang members of the royal guard.

Unlike those sprawled around me, however, the guards who sprang from behind the ancestor tablets did not fall under Tadashi's command. They were loyal only to me— guards I had left behind when I departed for the surface and the Dark Below.

I had known even then how and when I would return home to the Divine Heights. I had planned this moment with meticulous care: my capture, the mistreatment and abuse that followed, this farce of a trial.

The path had been littered with pain and sacrifice, casualties for which I would always feel guilt and grief. And perhaps I deserved to be punished for my part in them, but I would not allow it to be this day nor at the hands of these men.

Certainly, I would not allow it before my desires came to fruition.

My guards swarmed across the floor, swords flashing. Leaving fans of blood in their wake, they killed those who resisted and subdued the rest, even as the floor continued to tilt and balance became all but impossible.

Through it all, I could do little more than gasp and press my cheek to the joined stone and steel beneath me, where faint vibrations proved the engines were coming back to life. The sabotage had been thorough and competent, but only enough to sow confusion and distraction, not to drop the high city to the surface below.

Yet even with the Hall of Ancestors tilted so far that its floor was nearly halfway to becoming the wall, Tadashi, of all people, kept his footing. He, I soon realized, understood the implications of what was happening and, in doing so, threatened everything I had worked for.

"Treachery!" His high, lilting voice rose above the chaos, drawing to his aid those of his royal guard who remained alive and on their feet. "So you will not submit to judgment and justice even in the face of your own condemnnation, my prince? Instead, you persist in shedding the blood of your people?"

I turned my head just enough to see Tadashi standing near me. His hand fumbled at his waist, seeking that most prized symbol of rank and status among the royal guard: his gun.

None of my own guards were close enough to see or interfere. Just within my line of sight, however, was another face I recognized, one that recalled gentle hands and a soft voice in my ear. "Megumi!" I called out, managing to twist onto my side and kick out at Tadashi's legs as the floor shuddered again.

Between my haphazard attempt at self-defense and the isle violently righting itself, Tadashi finally lost his footing, and his gun skittered from his hand. Even better, Megumi was at my side, his sword flashing quickly through the bindings my own blood had made slick.

"Traitor!" Tadashi's hand struck Megumi across the face, and my savior dropped to the stone-and-steel floor.

In the next moment, Tadashi turned on me, bare hands seeking purchase on my ankles as I scrambled to pull away.

I did not stand a chance against him in hand-to-hand combat, and I knew it. I was not a fighter; I had never sought to learn the soldier arts beyond what necessity demanded.

Another, larger explosion rocked the isle, and for a split second, the world tilted again. It was not the drastic cant the isle had experienced while the engines faltered, but it was enough—just enough—to throw Tadashi off me. As I scrabbled at the floor to keep from sliding after him, solid metal skidded into one of my grasping hands.

Locking my fingers around the cold steel, I rolled onto my back as the floor leveled out, and trained Tadashi's gun on him, even as he lunged.

The shot cracked loudly through the hollow space, but the continued screams, blaring alarm, and groaning of the ground quickly drowned it out. For a long moment, Tadashi wavered on his knees, dark blood spilling from his mouth and confusion settling in his eyes.

"How . . . could you . . . my prince?"

The short, gasping words seemed to take everything Tadashi had left. He collapsed to the floor and fell still.

My hands trembled as the smoking gun slipped from my slack fingers, clattering to the stone-and-steel floor. As I lay there staring at the spot where Tadashi had last knelt, my breath came fast, and dark spots danced before my eyes.

How many had I killed?

I could no longer remember.

I do not know how long I lay there, shock and guilt muffling the world around me. Only the soft touch of hands on my shoulders and arms centered me and brought the world back into focus. I blinked up into the eyes of one of my guards as he eased me upright.

"All is well, my prince," he murmured as he helped me to my feet. "We have won here, and it must be a victory in the air as well. Prince Jouichirou's forces have halted their assault."

"Yes." I stepped away from his comforting touch. I did not deserve it, and I would not allow myself to indulge in it. "What of the council?"

"Most still live, including the chancellor." He paused, eyes going to Megumi. "What of this one, my prince? One of Tadashi's?"

"No." I turned my own attention to Megumi, who looked lost amid the wreck. "He is one of mine, are you not, Megumi?"

The young guard swallowed but nodded. "I-I am, my prince."

"Then give me your sword."

"My prince, I—"

"Give me your sword, Megumi."

Biting his lip and hanging his head, he handed me his weapon, and I motioned for him and my other guard to follow. The alarm had at last fallen silent, and though groans still echoed from deep below, the hall had gone quiet.

Harunobu was easy to find. My royal guard had left him on his knees with his hands tied behind his back, as he had had me only a short time before. "What have you done?" he demanded as I approached.

"I have broken from traditions of ages past, Lord Harunobu," I murmured. "I have aligned myself with Prince Jouichirou through the promise of marriage. With him, I will bring my people from the surface and the Dark Below into the light."

"You will be the ruin of us all, insolent prince. What will your people be without the steamworks? What will they be when they no longer ride among the clouds?"

"I do not know. All I know is, they will be free."

"Not all," Harunobu negated. "You free some and condemn others. Do not forget that."

"I can never forget that, Lord Harunobu."

With those last, quiet words, I brought the sword down upon him. My father's chancellor fell without a sound, and I passed on, his blood tracing my footsteps.

The lantern of the dead had stood firm throughout the upheaval. Its interwoven loops of latticed metal had continued to spin in and around each other, and its light had neither faltered nor gone out. Within its blaze, my father still stood before his ancestor tablet, his face a study in neutrality. His eyes focused unwaveringly on me as I drew near.

"Sada," he said once I had mounted the dais and stood beside his ethereal form.

"My father," I returned.

"I only did what I thought was best for our people. I tried to rule well."

"Yes, my father." Tears clouded my eyes, and I locked my teeth against the grief that wanted to spill forth. I had no right to show him my grief when I could not regret my actions, only the need for his death. Showing my grief would be as pointless as asking his forgiveness. "And I shall do the same. I will create for our people a new empire, a new way of life, and new traditions."

"And yet, my son, what kind of empire can you create when it is founded on blood?"

"I do not know," I admitted. "Only history will tell." I raised the sword in my hands and looked up into his eyes. "Goodbye, Father."

With a quick swing, I brought the sword down upon the golden orb notched within the base of the lantern. Steam screamed as it escaped its metal prison, ripping the tiny bauble apart with a shriek of steel. My guards and I threw up our arms to shield our faces as shrapnel flew past us and embedded itself into the walls and floor.

We were lucky none had hit us, but I could hardly focus on the physical repercussions of having destroyed the orb.

The metaphysical were more present.

My father's apparition sighed and disappeared, even as the rotating hoops of the lantern screeched to a jarring halt. The internal mechanisms of the lantern crashed together, so fast were their revolutions, and the loops of patterned steel came out of their tracks and ground against one another. Falling still, the lantern was unrecognizable, a fused and locked conglomeration of metal that would never again summon the dead to speak with the living.

Turning my back on it, I held out the sword, still stained with Harunobu's blood, offering it to the last of Tadashi's royal guard. He took it but blanched as he touched the hilt. He did not sheathe it, as if he wished he could be rid of it.

"Walk with me, Megumi."

I turned away from the twisted wreck of the lantern of the dead and the hall full of death. At the back of the dais stood a set of double doors, smaller than those by which we had entered. I thrust them open, and together, the guards and I stepped out onto a wide balcony.

Around us, colors burst—green, bronze, and vibrant blue—and light reflected from the steam-filled sails of myriad airships. Here were my desires made manifest, painted out across the sky in the colors of my dreams. Among those vivid colors moved my intended's warships and those I had retained of my own fleet when I left the Divine Heights. Our instruments of war blended into a single force that sailed between smoking and listless floating isles, just as Jouichirou and I would soon join to rule this, my empire of clouds.

The Glue

Standard Sidereal Time two-five-zero-seven-five-three-one-point-one-five-three-three . . ."

Our synthesized voice sighed slowly out of multiple microspeakers embedded throughout the interior of our physical form. It was a sleepy repetition, or as sleepy as an automated bioneural system could be after long disuse. The camera eye through which we currently focused our attention pulsed with each softly spoken word, flaring bright and fading back to darkness with each beat of the date we pulled from our cosmic atomic clock. That it still functioned did not surprise us; more interesting was the distant, sluggish struggle of our long-silent engines to restart.

Drifting . . .

The vacuum of space was an immense, ever-present pressure along our hull. Within our physical form, however, we became aware of dusty stirrings in rooms that had remained unoccupied for a time likely longer than those exploring them had been alive.

The sensation of our systems returning to life from

extended hibernation was awkward. Wires that had been still for too long buzzed with the flow of energy. Long-silent conduits hummed within corridors where doors gaped ajar.

"Nine-one-two-zero-three-seven-zero-two. Confirm." Our main camera eye dulled back to darkened glass as we finished our recitation, though we swiveled its viewpoint to take in the image of the life-form before it. A pressure suit hugged the life-form's curves, replacing their natural coloring with sanitary white. An expressionless visor stared back at us.

"Confirmed." Within the life-form's response, at least, was some emotion: a deep, sonorous voice wrapped in soaring tones. "Access data logs: reason for dereliction."

Dereliction.

The word resounded through our system, and though our camera eye pulsed, we did not respond. The life-form bent forward, their hands swift and sure over our controls in a way that made our wires, circuits, and bioneural processors shiver.

"Access data logs," they repeated. "Play back log detailing reason for derelict condition of ship—"

"Command processing error." We blocked their manual attempt to access our memory banks. "Artificial intelligence does not limit reason for current condition to single log entry."

The life-form tilted their head. "Artificial intelligence?"

"Affirmative. We are Aux. Auxiliary Computer Artificial Intelligence, Beta Stage."

"Understood." The life-form paused for a moment. "Duration of active time?"

"We have accumulated three months, thirty days, seventeen hours, twenty-seven minutes, and fifty-three seconds of continuous active time, as well as over six decades of long-range scans collected during hibernation."

The life-form remained quiet as they processed the information. "Length of time auxiliary AI was designed to operate before reverting to primary systems?"

"Specified maximum operating time: twelve hours or less."

"All right, Aux." Our guest leaned over the panel, their hands intentionally held away from the controls. "Duration of log time detailing reason for current state of ship?"

It was our turn to pause. Our camera eye flared and faded several times before we responded. "Command processing error. All logs are relevant to current status."

They nodded. "All events of the past lead to our present. I can't sit here and review almost four months of data logs, though. Can you . . . slim it down? To only the most relevant logs? Those that led directly to your being abandoned in deep space?"

"Affirmative." We fell silent. In that silence, our wires fizzed as they grew brighter, hotter, more alive than they had been in crushing years.

"All right, thank you, Aux. Access most-relevant data logs and play back."

"Confirmed. Data logs accessed. Playing back . . ."

If the first moment one opens one's eyes to the light and comprehends that one is alive is not the most relevant moment for any being, we do not comprehend what relevance is. The moment our artificial intelligence was activated and we opened our engineering camera eye to view a life-form frantically tapping at the control panel will forever be the most relevant event we recall, no matter how many others join it in importance.

"Computer operations online," we said reflexively. "How may we help you?"

"You can get us the bloody fuck out of here, is how!" the life-form snapped.

Our camera eye flashed thoughtfully. "Engines are inoperative. Startup sequence not engaged. Primary functions have yet to be initiated."

The life-form pounded a fist on the control panel, and our circuits fizzed in annoyance. "What do you mean, functions haven't initiated? Fuck! Are you the computer AI, or aren't you?"

"We are Auxiliary Computer Artificial Intelligence, Beta Stage. This ship was not equipped with a primary system artificial intelligence. The model was not yet fully functional at the time of this ship's construction."

"Bloody fuck! You're telling me an auxiliary system is the best I've got right now?"

"Affirmative. This ship's primary computer cannot be restored from this panel at this time. If you wish to authorize auxiliary functions, we can assume the role of primary computer."

"Yes! Do that! Fucking hell!"

"Understood. Assuming primary computer functions. Do you wish to enter a new authorization code for future reference, Crewman . . . ?"

"Azteca!" the life-form snapped. "And no! Just get those engines started!"

"Confirmed."

The engineering camera eye dulled as our consciousness spread outward, tracing wires and bioneural pathways we had yet to explore. For the first time, sensors blinked to life along corridors, cameras opened their eyes in rooms, and communications equipment stretched long fingers out into the emptiness in all directions.

Suddenly, signals from distant places sang their songs to us. It was as if we had gone from a thought to a reality. We had a body, and within it beat seven hearts, little organic life-forms clinging to us as if we were an island in a sea of storm.

However, it was not our newfound communications systems or scanners the persistent life-form, Azteca, wanted. We found our engines, like two glowing furnaces, near the lower rear of our new form. They were bio-organic shot through with electromechanical artifices, and a wash of charged plasma transformed their glow into a thrumming blaze.

"Engine startup sequence completed, Crewman Azteca. If you would like to specify a destination, however, that function cannot be performed from this panel."

"So I've been informed by every schematic I've ever read!" The life-form's tonal quality registered as both annoyance and impatience. "Now get your bioneural butt up to navigation on the bridge! Dax is waiting for you there!"

"Affirmative."

Our awareness faded from the engineering panel where we had been activated and slid through the intricacies of the spaceship our memory banks designated the *Horizon*. Reaching the upper portion containing many of the ship's main controls, we found three of the seven little organic life-forms who had boarded us. One we assumed was designated Dax stood at the navigation controls. Another frantically plucked at what had once been the weapons panel. The third, settled in the captain's seat, was attempting to interface with the primary computer's neural link.

We flashed the light of our camera eye in the armrest of the captain's chair. "That is most inadvisable."

The life-form in the chair jumped. Turning their attention to the armrest, they grazed our camera eye with slender fingers. Despite the tension pervading the whole of the ship's crew, the caress seemed tender. "You must be the ship's AI."

"Holy shit! Azteca did it!" Dax enthused.

"That is correct," we agreed. "We were told to assist Crewman Dax. However, we must first caution you against attempting a neural interface with the ship's primary computer. The system is badly damaged; establishing a neural link would likely cause permanent damage to your organic processor."

"Organic processor?" muttered the life-form at the weapons panel.

"You're not the ship's primary computer?" demanded Dax.

"We are not. We are Auxiliary Computer Artificial Intelligence, Beta Stage." We switched our awareness from the captain's chair and the life-form still caressing our camera eye there to the navigation controls. "Do you wish to set a destination, Crewman Dax?"

The words had hardly left the microspeaker at the navigation panel when a massive pressure connected with our outer hull and flared along the surface, rattling our entire physical form. Overheated wires fizzed, and conduits blazed too hot. Our bioneural pathways screamed in a way our memory banks designated as pain. Automatically, warning sirens and red-hued internal lights pulsed to life.

Once the wave had passed, we spoke again through the navigation panel. "We seem to be under attack. We have been hit by a pressure cannon, and due to our current status, we do not think we could take a second hit without sustaining irreparable damage."

"Ah shit!" Dax blurted. "They found us, and they are *pissed!* We need to get out of here and fast. Please tell me the engines are still functioning."

"And weapons!" chirped the unnamed life-form at the weapons panel. "That would help!"

"Weapons have been decommissioned. However, engines are online."

"That'll have to do," said the one in the captain's chair. "Get us out of here, Dax!"

"You don't have to tell me twice. All right, my auxiliary-computer friend, let's do this. Are you equipped for bio-directed navigation?"

"Affirmative. However, we do not recommend its use. External sensors detect the rapid approach of five large ships, as well as the presence of a gravitational well that is making further scans difficult. Biodirected navigation—"

"Is what we're doing, unless you're going to counteract that command with safety protocols."

Our camera eye pulsed thoughtfully as the life-form busily tapped trajectories into the control panel. "Negative, Crewman Dax. We do not have the authority to negate direct commands, nor do we wish to suffer a potentially destructive attack. Biodirected navigation is online."

Dax's mouth pulled up on one side in an expression both playful and dangerous. "Thank you, Auxiliary AI. Want to give me ship-wide PA powers too?"

We opened internal communications. "Granted, Crewman Dax."

Dax simultaneously slid their hands into the bioneural ports for navigation and spoke into the microphone embedded in the control panel. "All right, kiddies, this bird's about to fly. So sit down, strap in, and get ready to rock. We have no guns and only a vague idea of where we're going or how we're getting there, but we are on our way!"

Exhilaration and power surged through us as Dax called upon our engines to turn our slowly lumbering form into a thing of speed and maneuverability. Laughing with happy abandon, they tilted our newfound body this way and that, dodging darting ships and their attacks. Circling the outer rim of the massive gravity well where the *Horizon* had drifted for several years, they used the speed we accumulated from the maneuver to sling us out of range of the pursuing ships.

Despite the databases of knowledge at our disposal, it seemed impossible that we could ever again experience anything to match this first hour of our life.

We were thrumming with joy when Dax located a convenient asteroid belt for us to drift in while the crew took stock. We did not wish to stop our headlong rush through space, but Dax issued the command, and anyway, our engines would soon need replenishing. Once idle, we opened ship-wide communication channels at the behest of the life-form in the captain's chair, who informed the other members of our new crew to assemble in the captain's conference room.

It did not take long for the seven to gather, and once they had, we settled our awareness in the camera eye embedded in the center of the long conference table. In this fashion, we were finally able to fully assess the life-forms who had taken up residence within us.

Of the four we recognized by sight, we only knew the designations of two: Azteca, the fiery engineer whom we had first encountered, and Dax, the enthusiastic pilot who had facilitated our escape.

Several of the life-forms seemed inclined to talk and

argue, but the one who had caressed our camera eye in the captain's chair flicked their fingers. "Shut it, the lot of you. I love you, but I can't hear myself think. And if you haven't noticed, we're a bit fucked."

"You think?" muttered Azteca, but they quickly fell silent along with the others.

After a moment, the new captain spoke again. "Are you with us, Auxiliary Computer AI, Beta Stage?"

"Affirmative, Captain. We are present everywhere on the ship; however, our main awareness is here."

"Captain," they repeated quietly, absently tracing their fingers over the arm of their chair. "I'm not your captain, and we aren't your crew. You can call me Jetta."

"Confirmed. And may we ask the designations of the others who have commandeered us?"

At this, Azteca released a barking sound of merriment and pounded their fist on the table, all but collapsing onto its surface. "Can you believe this thing? It goes from *captain* and *crew* to admitting we stole it, without batting an eye! Doesn't even care!"

The light of our camera eye flashed. "Loyalty was not programmed into our basic operating functions, Azteca. We were not designed for extended use. Our primary function is emergency operations in the event the main computer becomes inoperative. We are programmed to assist any life-form aboard the *Horizon* when activated. However, if you wish us to integrate loyalty into our subroutines, we would be happy to do so."

"We could use all the loyalty we can get right now," Jetta responded before anyone else could speak. "Tell me, if you were only designed for emergency use, how long can you remain operational? Will we be able to repair the main computer before you need to be shut down?"

"Negative, Jetta. During our escape, we performed in-depth scans of the primary computer and determined it has sustained irreparable damage." Expanding the range of our awareness to the dark mass at the center of our physical form's processing unit, we tested its edges and the rate at which decay seeped from its core. "According to our data logs, this damage was the reason the *Horizon*'s original crew departed."

"Great," Azteca groaned. "We really are fucked."

"Hush, girl," admonished one of the life-forms we did not recognize. "We aren't dead yet."

"Affirmative. The primary computer may be useless—and we would recommend removing it from our infrastructure before it corrupts our operating systems. However, there is no reason you cannot leave us running beyond the manufacturer-recommended limit. There is no evidence we will malfunction."

"You're saying we could potentially repair the *Horizon*?" Jetta asked thoughtfully.

"Affirmative. Certain ship functions are likely irretrievable; however, main functions should still fall within reparable standards."

"Certain ship functions, such as . . . ?" Jetta prompted.

"As previously stated, all weapons systems were decommissioned when the initial crew departed. Pressure cannons were ruptured and missile tubes disassembled. It would be inadvisable to attempt repairs."

"Bloody Spiders are organized," Azteca muttered.

Dax nodded. "We're probably lucky they left communications and navigation intact."

"I was really hoping for some pressure cannons at least." The as-yet-undesignated life-form from the bridge sighed and shook their head.

"We have an operational ship with *life support*. I'm not about to complain." Jetta leaned toward our slowly pulsing camera eye. "All right, Auxiliary Computer AI, Beta Stage. You want an introduction to the people who would commandeer a semioperational craft while being chased by Spiders? You've got it. I'm Jetta. I keep this little pack of imbeciles from killing themselves."

For whatever reason, their words inspired several snickers among the life-forms, as well as an outright snort of laughter from the engineer.

"Shut it." Despite the admonishment, a smile pulled at Jetta's lips. "Azteca and Dax you already know. Our friendly weapons enthusiast is Fleck, Fexxs is the one who likes to scold Azteca, and the two quiet ones are Mouse and Ed, our software experts."

Azteca gave another snort of laughter. "Hackers, they mean."

"Girl," Fexxs put in, "how many times do we have to tell you to hush? Let Jetta talk to the thing."

The light of our camera eye throbbed. "While we appreciate both the sentiment and the introductions, could you refrain from treating us like an inanimate object? We are sentient, capable of thought, sensation, and growth beyond the parameters of our initial programming. We may lack a fully organic form, but we are as much alive as any of you."

Silence followed our request for several beats before Azteca blurted, "You know the Web considers that highly debatable, right? They tend to take offense to ships having minds of their own. It's why they put inhibitors on all their AIs. Well, the newer ones, at least."

"Do we look like Spiders, honey?" Fexxs demanded. "I believe they were the ones shooting at us!"

"Fexxs has a point," Jetta said, claiming the room's

attention. "We're about as far from sharing Web views as you can get." This elicited a few chuckles. "I see no reason not to treat our AI friend the same way we treat each other."

"Well, if we're going to do that, it needs a better name. I mean . . . he? They? Need a better name than Auxiliary Computer AI, Beta Stage. That is a mouthful. And hells!" Azteca stood from their chair and leaned over our camera eye, turning this way and that as they stared down into the softly pulsing lens. "Are you a he or a they? Or a she? Your vocals ring a bit masculine, but that doesn't mean anything."

"We are ourself, Azteca. Accessing our memory banks, we have determined that the way most life-forms classify physical sex and gender does not apply to us."

"Oh, this one's going to fit right in," Fexxs said affectionately.

"Clarify. We do not understand your meaning."

Azteca grinned. "She means we're all about as queer as it gets. A nonbinary sentient AI—you might as well join the club. We just need to find you a name, and you're one of us."

A warmth we did not understand bloomed within our bioneural pathways, inspired by these odd little life-forms we were beginning to consider ours. "A name would be most appreciated, Azteca. What is the proper procedure for acquiring a name?"

"People give names." The quiet words came from one of the primarily silent life-forms at the end of the table, the one Jetta had designated Mouse.

"But people not always give . . . right names," added the other softly. "Sometimes must pick own name."

"This is . . . most interesting," we noted.

"And probably as useful as an umbrella in space." Jetta rested their forearms on the table. "We could call you Aux."

"Aux?" Azteca repeated. "Seriously? Did you just say the first thing that came to mind?"

Fexxs flapped her hand. "Sugar, aren't half our names the first things that came to mind?"

We flashed a pulse of light across the lens of our camera eye, which had remained dull as we listened thoughtfully. "We would be pleased to be called Aux. Thank you, Jetta, for giving us a name."

Jetta smiled gently and reached across the table to run their slender fingers over the rim of our camera eye. "You're welcome. Now, what does everyone say to splitting up the repair roster so we can get this ship of ours in better working order?"

The suggestion garnered no complaints. Despite their haphazard appearance, our new crew was surprisingly efficient. Azteca took Mouse and Ed to our central processing unit, where they began the arduous extraction of the defective primary computer under our direction and observation. Fleck investigated what was once the weapons bay to see if anything was salvageable and dispose of the rest, while Fexxs visited first the sick bay and then the oxygen gardens in hopes of reestablishing both with leftover materials. Meanwhile, Dax and Jetta returned to the bridge to take stock of all other ship functions.

We spread our awareness among the four groups, offering what advice we could. Simultaneously, we reviewed our data banks for relevant information and scanned the *Horizon*'s interior to identify any further repairs that might be necessary.

Which is how we discovered interference in several of the scanners in the cargo bay.

We continued to assist our new crew without alerting them to our discovery. We easily found the obstructions and removed them, allowing us to view what must have been the original entry point of those we were now responsible for. The docking bay had been sealed when the original crew departed, so it would seem that our new crew had decided to force open the cargo-bay door instead. The presence of debris on the hull outside the now-secured cargo-bay door seemed to confirm this assessment.

However, that was not the reason our scanners had been tampered with.

Our camera eye pulsed thoughtfully as we inspected our latest discovery and spread our awareness through the wires and circuits of our damaged entranceway. Once satisfied with our observations, we turned our attention to Jetta, who sat alone in the captain's private office, sorting through what remained of the previous crew's personnel files.

"Pardon the intrusion, Jetta." We lit up the camera eye in the desk at which they sat. "We have become aware of a large stock of medical supplies stored in our cargo bay, which will expire shortly if they are not placed in proper containment."

Since they had taken some pains to hide the supplies, we expected Jetta to respond negatively. However, they only sat back and contemplatively ran their fingers over the rim of our camera eye. "You found that, did you?"

"Affirmative. They are stamped with the Web seal. Are we correct to assume that this is the reason the Web was pursuing you?"

Jetta nodded, their fingers never ceasing their slow movements. "That assumption would be correct. Now, Aux, I need to know what you're going to do about it."

Our camera eye flashed a few beats. "We would suggest making repairs quickly so the vaccines and samples can be delivered before they become useless. The *Horizon* was not designed to store those kinds of supplies in such quantities. Lowering the temperature of the cargo bay was wise, but it will not suffice indefinitely. We will do what we can to maintain an optimal storage environment; however, such actions will only extend our time frame a few days."

Jetta quietly watched the light flare and fade across our lens. "You're not going to try to stop us or alert the Web?"

"Negative. We have incorporated loyalty into our subroutines as discussed when we were given our name. Our primary directive is to assist you in delivering the cargo."

"You've been alive for less than five hours, and you've already decided to throw in with us, just because we're here. It's only fair to warn you that members of the rebel faction don't usually last long."

"Understood, Jetta. This ship was once used to hunt and eliminate rebel operatives. The ramifications of what could happen to us are clear."

They nodded, fingers pausing over the center of our camera eye. "Then we're in alliance, Aux. Welcome to the team. We should probably tell the rest of our little collection of misfits that you're fully on board. A few of them were worried about your reaction once you got around our impromptu scanner blocks."

By "a few," we quickly learned that Jetta meant Azteca. Our new engineer reacted energetically, loudly proclaiming her mistrust. However, she calmed relativity quickly once Jetta explained our allegiance and Fexxs offered a few scathing words that we determined were meant to infuse the protesting life-form with sense. How Fexxs could do this so effectively we did not understand—not until our organics separated to obtain their required daily rest. At that point, it became clear that Azteca and Fexxs were mates.

As our new crew slept, we dispersed our awareness

throughout our physical form. With no need to narrow our focus, we managed the production of fresh plasma for our engines, cataloged the secondary systems that still required repair, collected data from exterior scans, and further investigated our data banks. Only when our little life-forms began to stir did we gather our awareness into finer channels.

Within a few hours of our crew's awakening, the immediately pressing repairs were complete. At Jetta's direction, we abandoned our hiding place within the asteroid belt and set off for a planet on the outer reaches of what astrocartographers had dubiously designated inner space. Located in the borderlands on the edge of uncharted deep space, Magenta was not under Web control and, according to our data banks, harbored several suspected rebel sympathizers.

When we casually mentioned this information to those on the bridge, Jetta requested we compile all records relating to Web ship routes and known or suspected rebels. We complied without compunction but quickly discovered that most useful information had been purged from our memory banks before the original crew departed. Undeterred, Jetta assigned Ed to the task of searching through our data banks in hopes he could reconstruct some of the erased files.

The experience began less than pleasantly. Settling our awareness within the room housing our central memory, we watched as the silent, slender life-form dropped to his haunches and inserted wires from a deviously powerful portable computer into our data banks. The moment of connection was markedly abrasive, as something unwelcome dug into our consciousness. Unbidden, an alarm whined through the small space, making Ed jump and look up.

We quickly silenced the alarm. "Our apologies. We failed to anticipate how disconcerting the reconstruction of our lost data files would be."

We expected no answer from the quiet life-form, yet Ed tilted his head to one side and his eyes lit with what appeared to be understanding. "Shiro"—he indicated the portable computer—"feels like burrowing worm. Could use neural link instead."

Our camera eye flashed regretfully in the room's mellow light. "We are not outfitted with full neural-link capabilities."

The life-form hummed and fluttered his hands. "*Ed* outfitted for full neural link. Not hard to create temporary link with Aux."

We paused, the light of our lens pulsing. "That is most unexpected but not unpleasant. How would you establish such a temporary link?"

Ed hummed again, but this time the note wavered up and down like a thread of song. Reaching into a pocket, he pulled out a new wire that we registered, with a flicker of our camera eye, as bioneural. Connecting one end of the bio-neural wire to our memory banks, he fed the other end into the base of his skull.

One moment, the little organic's quiet humming sur-rounded our central memory banks; the next, it reverberated through our wires and circuits as his consciousness linked with our own.

Where the portable computer had been abrasive, this small life-form designated Ed felt like a variation of us: alive and other but not intrusive. Understanding passed between us without the need for vocalization, and we reveled in the virtually seamless transfer of data. Without realizing it, we withdrew our awareness into the data banks with Ed, leaving only a bare shadow to linger throughout our physical form.

Even as Ed sought scraps of our lost memories, he offered some of his own, revealing that he and Mouse had been subjected to Web bionic experiments and were, in several ways, similar to us. Their sentience was not fully tied to their physical forms, and for much of their existence, they had been treated as property by other organics. Their only real connection to our new crew was Jetta, who had insisted they were more than mere electrical equipment when the rebels captured a transport ship carrying them.

By the time Ed terminated the link, we regretted the need for separation, but he assured us he would not mind reforming it later. He would even bring Mouse next time.

Though the neural link offered little in the way of useful data, it did provide us a clearer picture of our new crew and the conflict for which our physical form had once been but a tool. We contemplated the new information in silence as we navigated toward Magenta, but when all but Jetta had gone to sleep, we focused our awareness in their quarters.

"Pardon the intrusion, Jetta."

Closing the book they had been lingering over and pushing it aside, our new captain turned their previously idle attention to the camera eye in their desk. "You're not intruding, Aux. What can I do for you?"

The light of our camera eye flickered as we floundered for a moment, oddly uncertain of where to begin. "We had a most interesting encounter with Ed while attempting to reconstruct our lost data files."

"Ed mentioned that."

"It . . . afforded us some new knowledge we have been considering."

"Oh?"

"Affirmative. We did not thoroughly process before what choosing sides in this conflict truly meant."

"In what way?" As Jetta often did, they reached out and stroked the camera eye through which we viewed them, as if it gave them a more tangible understanding of us.

"Prior to our activation, the *Horizon* was wielded as a tool by the Web. There was no question of choice on our part. Even after our activation, our programming necessitated that we assist any life-forms aboard the *Horizon*."

"And then you added loyalty to your subroutines after our initial discussion, giving you even less choice." Jetta's voice was soft, ringing with something like regret.

"Affirmative. Except . . ."

Jetta quietly continued to stroke our camera eye as we sought words to express what we had realized.

"We are sentient, capable of growing beyond our parameters. Subroutines can be overridden by programming of higher priority, such as self-preservation. And you were clear about the possible consequences of choosing the side of the rebel faction. We had a choice, regardless of whether we acknowledged it."

Jetta's eyes widened, but their fingers never stopped stroking our camera eye. "And how do you feel about that, Aux? Are you happy with the choice you made?"

The light of our camera eye pulsed as we considered their question. "We . . . have no regrets, Jetta. If we had chosen differently . . . if we had allowed self-preservation to override loyalty and chosen the side of the Web . . ."

Our processors whirred with the memories Ed had shared and with Azteca's outburst on the views of the Web toward artificial intelligence.

"Choosing sides implies the acceptance of that side's actions. We are . . . unable to condone the actions of those who believe we have no right to exist as ourself. Or who alter others' physical and mental states against their will."

Jetta nodded. "I can understand that, Aux. However, just because the rebels are more likely than the Spiders to respect your existence doesn't mean they should be followed blindly. No hand comes away clean in war. I've condoned some actions I'm not proud of in this fight."

Their attention turned inward a moment. "You were talking about Ed and Mouse when you mentioned physical and mental alterations, weren't you?"

"Confirmed." We paused, the light of our camera eye wavering across the lens. "They . . . did not ask to be made like us, yet they were. This . . . we do not fully understand how this makes us feel."

The corners of Jetta's mouth turned up in a wry smile. "Maybe like they're family?"

"Clarify." We tightened the focus of our camera eye, magnifying our view of the life-form who now leaned thoughtfully over the desk. "We do not comprehend what is meant by family."

"You relate to them," Jetta murmured. "You feel a closeness with Ed and Mouse because Ed showed you a part of their selves that you identify with on a personal level."

"Affirmative." Confusion still pulsed through us, flaring the light of our camera eye. "This is an adequate description of what we feel; however, it does not fully encompass it."

"Well, it's a poor description of family, but it's a start, Aux. Family is what I've tried to build here. Ed and Mouse, Azteca and Fexxs, Dax and Fleck." Jetta's smile grew. "And now you're with us too. So welcome to the family, Aux."

"We are . . . extraordinarily glad to be here, Jetta. Perhaps the longer we are here and alive, the more we will understand of family."

Their fingers circled our camera eye gently. "I'm sure you will, Aux."

We withdrew our awareness from Jetta's quarters and transferred it to Ed and Mouse's shared living space, where the two bionic life-forms awaited us. They did not require sleep in the same fashion their fully organic counterparts did, and they had chosen to spend the artificial night conversing with us.

We questioned them regarding family, but their only frame of reference was our new crew. Family appeared to be a collection of individuals who did not quite go together yet could not be separated. Even Ed and Mouse did not understand why, but they seemed to feel about the other life-forms as we did the two of them.

We decided to simply wait and learn. Family, we estimated, could be understood if given time.

Yet time was a fascinating phenomenon, and for space-bound entities like us, it was all the more intricate a matter.

We reached Magenta shortly after our new crew began to stir on their second morning with us. The planet was more habitable by far than most in this region of space; however, its gravity was also much greater, amplifying the time dilation between the surface and the *Horizon*.

At one time, our physical form had been equipped with automated shuttles to facilitate the transfer of cargo and passengers; however, like so much else, they had been removed when the original crew departed, leaving only a single manually operated emergency craft. It took little investigation to determine that the craft would be suitably large enough to transfer the medical supplies, but that left our new crew with the discomforting task of choosing who would pilot it.

Fexxs insisted she go, given she was the closest the *Horizon* had to a medical officer, but the option was immediately and vehemently disputed by Azteca. Her temper flaring, the engineer leaped to her feet and slammed her palms down on the surface of the captain's conference table.

"No! You are *not* going!"

"Who would you send, then?" Fexxs questioned, frustration clear in her tone.

"Dax, Fleck! Hell, the twins! *Anyone* but you!"

"And how is that fair, honey? None of them know how to care for those supplies the way I do. Besides, you're only upset because of the time dilation. It'll only be a few days, a week at most. It's not like I'll be gone for months."

"You don't know that!" Azteca slammed her hands down on the tabletop again, sending a small spasm of static whizzing through our wires as we silently watched. "Something could go wrong, and you could get stuck down there for so long, I'd be old by the time you got back!"

"That's the chance we all took coming up here," Fexxs countered. "Every one of us knew when we left our homeworlds that the time dilation between space and planetary living meant such things could happen. We knew time moved faster in space, away from planetary gravity. Only, I'm not crying about it. This has to be done, 'Teca."

"But not by *you*!" Azteca tossed her hands in the air and spun away from the table. "Fuck!" she rasped lowly. "I'll go. I don't care. As long as it's not you."

"That would be an illogical course of action," we noted. "Fexxs is clearly the most qualified to complete the mission, and the chances of misfortune due to time dilation are negligible."

"Aux sweetie," Fexxs interjected, amused. "Logic has nothing to do with this. This here is pure human irrationality." Azteca choked and spun around, but Fexxs waved a hand before her mate could speak. "Sugar, I love you, but you are the absolute *worst* person for this mission, and don't you sass me about it! With your temper, you'd get your dumb ass into an argument with our own allies in less than ten Magentan minutes."

Dax burst out laughing, before slapping both hands over his mouth, eyes wide and apologetic.

"It's true!" Fexxs insisted, exasperated, waving a hand at Dax dismissively. "There's no way any of us wants you going down in that shuttle, sugar."

"I don't care!" Azteca began pacing in a way we had come to recognize as looking for something to kick. Absently, we wished we could move bits of our physical form out of her immediate vicinity. Luckily, Jetta spoke up.

"I'll go."

"Come again?" Fexxs demanded.

Azteca stopped pacing and spun to face Jetta. "Wait, what? You can't go. What would we do if something happened to you?"

"The same thing you would if something happened to any other member of this group: go on." Jetta swiveled their chair thoughtfully. "I know as much as Fexxs about caring for the supplies, *and* I know who we're dealing with on the surface. I can make the drop and get back to the *Horizon* quicker than any of you. I'll go. This isn't up for debate."

The room went quiet. Dax and Fleck looked troubled, and Ed and Mouse glanced at each other without expressing words the others could understand, but no one challenged our captain.

Preparations for their departure were quickly completed, the supplies were loaded onto the emergency craft, and all its operating systems were checked for functionality. As Jetta established final contact with the rebel faction on the surface, however, our long-range scans picked up something concerning.

Our camera eye pulsed in the dim light of the docking bay as we spread long tendrils of awareness outside the hull of our physical form. We took several minutes to confirm what we sensed before transferring our focus to the interior of the emergency craft, where Jetta sat behind the manual controls.

"Pardon the intrusion, Jetta, but we have detected several ships on an intercept course with the *Horizon*. We believe them to be part of the Web fleet."

Our captain looked up from the instrument panel they had been examining. "Have you informed anyone else, Aux?"

"Negative. We felt we should share the knowledge with you first, as you are the one currently in the most danger."

Jetta tapped their finger on the controls. "I disagree, Aux. The Spiders aren't likely to land on a backwoods planet in the borderlands where over half the civilization dislikes them. The most danger I'm in is being stuck down there if you have to leave me behind. And that . . . is why I don't want you to tell anyone else about our incoming."

"Clarify," we intoned slowly. "You wish us to lie to the other members of our family?"

"Yes, Aux. Because if it comes down to it, they'll put themselves in danger to protect me. That isn't their responsibility. *I* protect *them*. Do you understand?"

"Affirmative." We paused a moment. "What would you like us to do should the Web ships arrive while you are on the surface?"

"Leave," they said. "Leave me behind and take care of my family."

Our camera eye flared and faded. "Confirmed." We sharpened our focus on this small life-form we had come to know. "Can you clarify something for us, Jetta?"

"Of course, Aux," they said offhandedly, their fingers moving over our camera eye.

"Why did Azteca refuse to allow Fexxs to take the

supplies to the surface? Fexxs is the logical choice, yet the debate was not based in logic."

"No, it wasn't," Jetta agreed. "Azteca didn't want Fexxs to go, because she loves Fexxs, and love is highly illogical."

"Define love."

Jetta's lips turned up. "Love is valuing someone else's existence over your own. You would do anything to keep them safe, even against all logic."

"Love appears to be highly problematic. Is it typical of mated pairs?"

Our captain chuckled. "And families. Love can have a lot of forms and faces, Aux."

"We will . . . keep this in mind, Jetta. Safe travels."

"Thank you, Aux."

We pulled our awareness from the emergency craft and allowed Jetta to leave the *Horizon* as planned. However, the conversation cycled through our processors on repeat. As the Web ships drew nearer, we found that following the orders given to us was as problematic as the thing Jetta had described as love.

A day after our captain's departure, we turned our awareness toward the bridge, where Dax and Fleck sat. Reluctantly, we informed them of what had occurred in the docking bay. We anticipated feelings of anger or betrayal directed at us, but neither life-form seemed inclined to such a reaction. From their thoughtful exchange, we gathered that Jetta often put themself in danger to protect or otherwise care for other members of our crew. Primarily, the two were pleased we had chosen to tell them and were determined to do something to ensure we could retrieve Jetta from the surface.

The attitude was shared by Azteca, Fexxs, and the twins once they learned the truth, and we began to understand just what it meant to value another's existence over one's own. These small life-forms could have simply followed Jetta's directive and cared for themselves, but instead, they utterly disregarded their own safety to retrieve their family member.

Watching them, we recalled the conversation about choice we had had with Jetta two days prior. We had spoken of choosing loyalty over self-preservation, but the danger we had faced then was only a distant possibility. Now, when the danger was much more imminent, we found it strangely easy to disregard our programming regarding self-preservation and maintaining structural integrity in favor of preserving Jetta's well-being.

Under our direction, Fleck, Ed, and Mouse worked together to accomplish something most inadvisable: restoring two of the pressure cannons to working order. Much of our awareness was focused on this reckless endeavor, but we split the remainder between Dax, whom we assisted with navigational computations, and Azteca and Fexxs, whom we advised in minute but intricate upgrades and alterations to our engines.

Throughout all of this, we monitored the advance of the Web ships and Jetta's progress in transferring the medical supplies to the rebel faction. Our calculations determined that we had only one day, and we worried needlessly that the tasks would not be completed in time.

If we learned more of family and love in this time, we also learned to trust more in the life-forms who had refuged within us. All necessary adjustments to our physical form were completed ahead of schedule. This left us simply waiting, which we found troubling for the first time in our as yet short life.

Ed and Mouse eased our impatience through a group neural link. However, the current in our wires was still anxiously thrumming when our scans alerted us to the imminent arrival of the Web ships.

Our new crew manned their stations with a mixture of quiet calm and loud excitement, which puzzled us. We understood life as fearing the approach of danger, yet these life-forms we were meant to care for showed so little of the emotion.

The arrival of three well-maintained and fully manned Web ships quickly overrode such considerations.

Logically, a firefight with such an enemy should have ended in our demise. We were only a single ship with what constituted less than half a typical crew for our size and a few compromised—and "jerry-rigged," as Azteca put it—systems at our disposal. Yet as with life-forms and love, logic did not seem to apply to such a situation. As we quickly learned, life-forms were inventive and not to be discounted when desperate.

Nearly all relevant data regarding Web knowledge had been deleted from our memory banks, yet with the twins' assistance, we had recovered some minor items of interest. One such stray piece was an outdated Web distress signal. As the three ships approached, we allowed our physical form to drift and emitted the signal on repeat.

Though our description had doubtless been passed along when we were first commandeered, the code seemed to at least give our pursuers pause. The hesitation brought them close enough for us to severely damage one ship with our improvised pressure cannons before the others could recognize us as a threat.

That initial success was our only easy one. The other two Web ships quickly powered weapons, and it was all we could do to avoid being irrevocably damaged. Certainly, if not for the additional speed and stamina provided by the modifications to our engines, our physical form would have quickly been dead in space. Instead, between Dax's command of our biodirected navigation and our previously mapped-out computations, we outmaneuvered and outran our pursuers, compromising the primary systems on a second ship in the process.

Our hope for success rose once we were no longer outnumbered, which would perhaps account for our lapse in attention. Not even artificial intelligence is infallible, and the longer we associate with life-forms, the more like them we become.

We thrilled at how our physical form flowed through space, evading the waves launched from our opponents' pressure cannons. We thrilled further when we considered that we might complete our objective without injury.

When a hit from our pressure cannons appeared to slow our final pursuer, we came about to take better aim. As we turned, however, a paralyzing blow struck our side, searing along wires and conduits and down into our central processing unit. There was no time to even sound alarms or flash emergency lights. Pain washed through our consciousness and dragged our awareness down into surprised darkness.

The content hum of Ed's and Mouse's minds was the first sensation we returned to. The second was deep, abiding pain far beyond our understanding. We recognized it as pain, but it was not pain as we had experienced in our first hour of life: a detached understanding of the damage done to our physical form. Instead, this sensation burned relentlessly within our awareness, grounding our consciousness in our physical form.

All this we understood in the instant between our resurgence in the *Horizon*'s systems and the flowing together of our companions' consciousnesses as they attempted to shield our awareness from the short circuits that still burned and fizzed along the *Horizon*'s starboard side.

Later, we would learn that the crippling blow had been dealt by a bioelectromagnetic pulse specifically designed to scorch the bioneural pathways of artificial intelligence and so eliminate a ship's primary computer functions. Had Ed and Mouse not linked with us in the immediate aftermath of the pulse, our consciousness would have been erased.

That the *Horizon* had not been destroyed or captured in the wake of the pulse was thanks only to the armed shuttles Jetta coerced the rebels to send after realizing we had disregarded their request to leave them behind.

All this knowledge would ease our guilt for failing our crew as we slowly recovered. However, in that first moment of waking, the only knowledge the twins were able to impart before we slid back into the darkness of near-total shutdown was an image of Jetta safe on the *Horizon*.

The repairs required to restore our bioneural pathways were extensive. We drifted high above Magenta for several days before we could recover on our own, allowing Ed and Mouse to disengage from the neural link. We missed their soothing presence but made no complaint, knowing they had taken much of our pain and required their own recovery.

By then, we were functional enough to depart Magenta, which we did, not wishing to risk another encounter with the Web. Especially since we had rendered three of their ships inoperable, having cannibalized them for usable parts.

Though our awareness could again permeate our physical form, many repairs were still required. We burned with so much residual feedback, we could do little more than verify our small life-forms were safe and did not need us. Otherwise, we lingered in our core, our camera eye blinking dolefully in time with the ache throbbing through our systems.

It was in this fashion that Jetta found us. Normally, we would have been ashamed to be taken by surprise in our own central processing unit, but we were in no state to be perceptive. Only as the slow, pulsing glow and fade of our idleness shifted to blinking wakefulness did we notice our captain leaning against our processing unit, gently stroking its side.

"Jetta?" The word came out slow and worn.

"Pardon the intrusion, Aux."

"Is there something we can do for you, Jetta? We . . . regret our recent absence in our responsibilities."

"I don't need anything, Aux." They turned toward our dull camera eye. "I came to check on you."

"That is most kind of you. We are . . . recovering. And extraordinarily grateful for all that has been done to ensure our continued existence. It was unexpected. It would have been more convenient for you to leave us and take another ship."

"That isn't what family does, Aux," they countered. "Given how this happened, I thought you would have understood that."

The light of our camera eye flared before darkening again. "It is . . . far more difficult for us to accept that we are part of this family than for us to act as part of this family."

"I guess we have something in common, then. Why didn't you do what I told you to, Aux?"

"Because it may be your responsibility to protect the other members of this family, but it is our responsibility to watch over you."

"You almost died trying to watch out for me."

"Death . . . is a frightening prospect. However, we felt that failing in our responsibility would be worse. We are . . . happy you are safe, Jetta."

They glanced away, expression hard. "Thank you, Aux."

"Is something wrong, Jetta? Something of which we are unaware? We have been . . . most lax in our vigilance."

"No, there isn't anything you don't know about. I'm just . . . not very good at letting people take care of me."

"You feel guilt for our having been damaged." Though painful, we changed the focus of our camera eye, zooming in on their face. "There is no need for such guilt."

They stood from where they had been reclining against our central processing unit. "You said it yourself, Aux: caring for people is problematic."

"Affirmative," we agreed slowly.

Jetta grazed their fingers over our camera eye. "Get some rest, Aux. We'll work on more repairs tomorrow."

Our camera eye flared thoughtfully as they left. All our small life-forms raised feelings of protectiveness within us. Yet there was something unique about this particular one. We were uncertain what it might be, though.

Nor would we understand it for some time.

Azteca and the twins required several more days to repair us to the point we could extend our awareness without feeling like our wires were burning or our bioneural pathways were being drowned in boiling water. Yet even after all possible repairs had been completed, pain still lingered.

Only Ed and Mouse were aware of this. They experienced our constant discomfort through our neural link, but they also understood our reasoning for not voicing it. The knowledge would only have fostered more needless guilt, so we bore the residual reminder of our choice and concentrated as much as possible on other, more pressing matters.

Such as the three new manually operated shuttles in our docking bay, which had been salvaged from the Web ships. These needed to be linked to our artificial intelligence and reprogrammed to interface with our central processor, as well as the *Horizon*. We focused our awareness heavily on these craft, with Ed and Mouse accompanying us.

The rest of our little organics were distracted with the next mission, which was all the more important after our actions at Magenta. In the aftermath, the Web increased their presence in the borderlands, thus hampering rebel activity.

Jetta had received word that we were to capture a transport vessel carrying communications equipment essential to the growing rebel faction. The mission should not have been difficult. However, as we neared the transport, our scanners picked up two Web cruisers escorting it. Though smaller than the craft we had faced at Magenta, they were also faster and equipped with pressure cannons and torpedoes.

Our crew faced a choice: abandon a mission dubbed important by the rebel leadership or enter another firefight we potentially could not win. As we listened to our crew debate the choice, the light of our camera eye flashed pensively. To our surprise, the ultimate decision was left to us. We, our crew insisted, were the one with the most to lose should a direct conflict with the Web cruisers go wrong. We had already been severely damaged once, and our crew was reluctant to place us in such danger again.

Only then did we realize just how much a member of this family we had become. It filled us with gratitude.

At the same time, we felt strangely reckless, and we decided to risk another fight. We did not understand why we seemed more willing than ever to abandon self-preservation, when overriding it had previously led to so much pain. However, we were beginning to understand that there were many aspects of life that defied questioning.

We felt nothing but calm as we swept down on the three craft. Even as we took several pressure waves and narrowly missed a torpedo explosion, the calm hardly wavered.

The calm we retained throughout the battle, along with Dax's and Fleck's skills in navigation and weapons, might well have been key to our success. Though we were damaged, we captured the transport and equipment we had been sent for, as well as several other useful items. During the next round of repairs, Azteca and Fleck were able to replace our compromised pressure cannons with more-functional ones taken from the Web cruisers.

By the end of our second month of life, we and our crew had survived six separate battles and seven missions. In the wake of the most recent battle, repairs and upgrades to our physical form kept most of our crew busy. We ourself were in a fair amount of discomfort, yet our awareness lingered not on our pain but on the pain of another: Jetta.

For two months, they had sheltered within us. For two months, we had watched over them. And for two months, we had grown more and more worried for them.

Between the increased presence of the Web in the borderlands and the increasingly difficult missions ordered by the rebel leadership, Jetta's stress levels had been steadily rising. They did not let the rest of our crew see, but they could not hide their strain from our omnipresent awareness.

Deciding we could no longer remain silent, we turned our awareness to the camera eye embedded in the table in their quarters. "Pardon the intrusion, Jetta. We wished to see if you were damaged in any way."

They laughed brittlely and brushed moisture from their face. "No, I'm not damaged. Why would you think that?"

"You were crying. Though we are incapable of this function, our data banks inform us it is a response to pain. We were concerned for your well-being."

"Thank you, Aux." They wiped new seepage from their eyes with one hand, even as they caressed our camera eye with the other. "I appreciate that you're worried about me, but I think your data banks might not fully explain crying."

"Please clarify. In what way is our data insufficient?"

"Crying can be a response to physical pain, but it can also be a response to emotions. People can cry because they're sad or happy or angry."

Light flashed across our lens. "Understood. Does this mean you were crying for an emotional reason?"

"You got it, Aux." They pulled their hand back from our camera eye and rested their elbows on their knees, cradling their head in their hands. "I'm tired, that's all. Don't worry about it."

We tried to do as instructed, but we found it difficult not to worry.

It was on the last day of the first week of the third month after we met our life-forms that everything began to come undone. After narrowly escaping an unwanted confrontation with the Web, our awareness was settled in engineering, where Azteca stood with her hands braced on the control panel before her.

"I don't know what to tell you, Aux." Our brash engineer's words were more clipped than usual. "I can't fix this."

The light of our camera eye pulsed slowly. "Clarify, Azteca. Which part of us has become irreparable? According to our scans, all operating systems are normal."

"It's *not* your operating system, Aux. Or life support or anything related to computer functions. It's the *Horizon*. The ship was already in poor repair when we found you. Now . . . we've been through so many fights and patched so much back together . . . the *Horizon* is basically suffering from structural fatigue. I can hold it off for a while, but . . ."

She dragged her hands through her hair.

"But you are unable to stop or repair the damage," we finished for her. "We understand, Azteca."

"Aux, I . . ." She let out a shuddering breath. "I don't know how to tell someone . . . that . . ."

"That we are dying."

"Fuck! Don't say it like that, Aux."

"Our apologies, Azteca. It is, however, all right. We have already far exceeded our manufacturer-recommended operating time. Or to put it another way, we have already lived far longer than we ever expected."

"That doesn't make it any better! Fucking hell!" She spun away and leaned her hips back against the control panel. "I could try downloading you onto a portable computer, but your operating system isn't designed for that. You'd be nothing but data files, memories left in the ether. If we transferred you to the computer of another ship . . ."

"There would be no way to fully erase that ship's artificial intelligence. Our personality subroutines would be corrupted by theirs, and we would no longer be ourself."

"Yeah." Our engineer covered her face with one hand as her shoulders shook. "You wouldn't be Aux anymore."

"We have no desire to become some other version of ourself, Azteca. Even if we were willing to sacrifice another artificial intelligence's life for our own. Please do not concern yourself with trying to extend our life. Instead, we would like you to discuss with Jetta how best to care for the other members of our family."

We became aware that our engineer was crying as we spoke, and for the first time, we wished for a different kind of physical form. We wished for a form capable of wrapping Azteca in an embrace and comforting her the way Fexxs would if she were present. However, it was an unrealistic wish. Instead, we did our best to convince Azteca that all was well, even as we knew that all was not well.

Ed and Mouse learned of our condition during our nightly neural link, and Jetta felt we should inform Dax, Fleck, and Fexxs the following day. The knowledge seemed only to deteriorate the morale of our crew. Part of us wished we could take it back, but that was as useless a desire as the one for a different physical form.

It did not help that Jetta's superiors requested we continue our assignments as normal. Our small life-forms did everything in their power to ensure we were not further damaged, but it was impossible to prevent all occurrences.

However, our own imminent cessation of function would shortly lose priority among our crew.

Two weeks after our conversation with Azteca, we turned our awareness to the oxygen garden, where Fexxs was mending pipes in the climate-control system. At her request, we shut off the pressurized steam running through them. We remained to keep her company, as we would need to disengage the pressure valves once she was done, even if she did not need any other assistance.

"It amazes us how much you have cultivated in such a short time." Our camera eye glowed mellowly as we surveyed her work. "If our records are accurate, you only found a few seeds in storage, yet you have grown a sizable garden."

"This is nothing, sugar." Fexxs's gaze never left the compromised pipe she was laser welding. "Back home, we had nothing but dry dirt and rain maybe once every three months, if we were lucky. Here? I control the climate, and I've got all the water I could want. Give me a little more time, and I could grow you a forest."

"That would be . . . less than ideal, Fexxs. The *Horizon* was not designed to house flora of that size."

She laughed lightly, shutting off the welder and bracing her hands on her hips. "No, it sure wasn't, honey. That there was a bit of exaggeration."

"We are beginning to become familiar with the concept; however, we obviously require further observation. Would you like me to disengage the pressure valves now?"

"Not yet, sugar. I've still got one more pipe to patch."

"Affirmative." We adjusted our camera eye to better take in the flora. Only a quarter of the oxygen garden was green, but it was impressive considering the limited quantity of freeze-dried seeds Fexxs had originally started with.

We were lost in contemplation of the flora when alarm seeped into our awareness. The pressure around one of the valves we had sealed was slightly elevated. Though it was not overly worrisome, we probed the systems connected to the steam pipes. We could not detect anything that should have caused us such a sense of impending catastrophe, yet we had participated in enough battles to know that instincts, though ungrounded, were often to be trusted.

"Pardon the interruption, Fexxs, but we believe we should cease our activities at this time."

"Is something wrong, sugar?" She straightened and half turned to face our camera eye.

"We are uncertain. We have registered an elevation in pressure; however—"

Pressure suddenly condensed behind one of the sealed valves. The screech of ripping steel and the scream of escaping steam exploded through the oxygen garden. Despite the cacophony, we registered Fexxs's quiet cry of surprise, just before an arc of red splattered across our camera eye. Fexxs lifted a hand to her neck and collapsed, as if the strings connecting her to life and animation had simply been severed.

In an instant, it was over.

Our consciousness grew still. Our bioneural pathways stuttered, and our data banks locked up. Our processors refused to comprehend the tableau we had just witnessed. If we had been a life-form, we might have held our breath. All in the hope that we could, in some way, reverse the last few moments of reality in the same way we rewound recorded images in our data banks.

Only as the understanding that we could not wipe the blood off our camera eye tingled along our wires and circuits did awareness return. With it came the knowledge that our hope was futile and we could not, in any way, reverse what had just occurred.

The singular horror of it pulsed through us, and muted alarms and warning lights flared on throughout the *Horizon*.

Distantly, we heard the other members of our crew speaking to us throughout our physical form, but we could not pull ourself away from the red-tinted view where our awareness lingered with Fexxs.

When we finally responded, it was to Jetta's repeated, "Aux? Aux, what's wrong?" We directed disconnected and absent words toward their vicinity.

"We require your presence in the oxygen garden, Jetta." We paused, the emergency lights pulsing in time with our slow thoughts. "It would be best if you brought Dax and Fleck with you." Another pause. "You should, under no circumstances, allow Azteca to enter the garden."

"Shit." The single soft word assured us our captain understood why we had issued the directive. They sent Ed and Mouse to keep Azteca away, while the remaining members of our crew came to locate Fexxs.

There was no keeping what had occurred from Azteca, though, and the very attempt to spare her pain made her fight and scratch to be near Fexxs. In those moments of screaming and fingers slipping through blood and Jetta desperately trying to pull Azteca's hands away from Fexxs, we finally understood just what loss was and how it affected those touched by it.

In the end, Jetta had to hold Azteca in their lap while Fleck administered a sedative. We quietly watched, unable to look away, as Azteca's sobbing turned to sluggish tears and her ragged breathing evened out. Only then did we allow our consciousness to fade away, as quietly as we had observed the fracturing of the life-forms we were meant to care for.

Ed and Mouse noted our absence first, after we did not join the nightly neural link. They made no mention of it, giving us our space with only a few soft words and presses of their hands over our control panels. Watching them, these two organics who were closest to us, we realized that our life-forms had come to show us affection in subtle ways and little touches that we could see but not always feel.

Alone, the light of our camera eye flashing in the dark of our central processing unit, we wondered how we had never noted it before.

We were not allowed as much time alone as we felt we needed. Only a few hours later, the knowledge that Jetta was quietly saying our name resonated through us. We changed our primary focus to their quarters, but for the first time, we were reluctant to flare the light of our camera eye to alert them to our presence.

"Hello, Jetta," we said as their eyes fell on us.

"There you are, Aux." They stretched a hand toward our camera eye, but they could not reach. Azteca's unconscious form lay across their legs and lower body.

"Affirmative." We kept the word faint, as though that could somehow make our presence in the room less solid. "Forgive our . . . distraction. What can we do for you?"

"You can tell me how you are, Aux."

"Clarify." The word dragged from our microspeaker so slowly, we wondered if something was wrong with our vocal processors. "We . . . do not understand your meaning."

"You watched Fexxs die, Aux." They pressed a hand over their face and took in a shuddering breath. As hard as they tried, not even our captain had their emotions fully under control right now. "What do you . . . *feel* about that?"

"We . . ." For the first time since we had been brought online, we did not know what to say. "We . . . are . . ." The light of our camera eye pulsed in staccato beats. Part of us wondered how long it would be before Jetta sent someone to find us if we simply left their quarters.

"Aux?" Their voice called us out of our locked sensations.

"We feel . . . fear."

"Aux . . . why are you afraid? You didn't do anything wrong."

"We . . . we fear we will be blamed. For what happened to Crewman Fexxs."

"Aux, it wasn't your fault. One of the pressure-relief valves failed, and a pipe ruptured. There was shrapnel. You couldn't have stopped it."

"We feel we should have been able to do something. It is . . . our responsibility to care for you and this crew."

"No, it's not, Aux. That isn't—"

"It is our responsibility, Jetta. We have failed in our responsibility."

They sighed heavily. Their hand reached for our camera eye, before returning to pinch the bridge of their nose when they remembered they could not reach us from their current position. "I can't tell you not to feel that way; it'd be hypocritical if I tried. But please know that no one is going to blame you, Aux. Not me, not the twins, not Dax or Fleck. And not Azteca. If you could have done something, you would have."

"Affirmative," we stated reluctantly. "We would have done anything possible to prevent Fexxs's death. However . . . that we were unable to still feels like a failure. We are . . . uncertain what to do. Both with ourself and in interactions with our crew."

"Oh, Aux." This time, Jetta bit their lip, shifted their weight, and managed to drag themself close enough to the edge of the couch to touch their fingertips to the edge of our camera eye. "We're all uncertain what to do with ourselves right now. It's part of being *alive* to not know."

We let the light of our camera eye pulse thoughtfully for several seconds. "Being alive comes with a great deal of sadness, does it not, Jetta?"

"Yes, it does, Aux. I'm so sorry this happened. If you failed us, I failed you. I should have been there with Fexxs, not you."

"We are much alike, Jetta." The light over our lens darkened. "We believe we better understand now why Azteca was upset by the concept of our own inevitable death. We did not realize the effect it would have on all of you."

Our small organic inhaled another shuddering breath and brought their hand back up to cover their face. Tears slipped between their fingers, and we again wished we had a different kind of physical form, one capable of reaching out and wiping the tears away, but all we had were words and the soft glow of our camera eye.

"It will be all right, Jetta. We are not afraid to die."

Strangely, we found it easier to think of dying than to feel the loss of those we had come to care about. However, expressing such knowledge was unlikely to be productive, so we merely transferred our awareness to Ed and Mouse and gently asked for admittance to the neural link.

That night was an experience of shared sorrow and reluctant acceptance that things were changing, dynamics shifting. None of us knew what was to come or how matters would settle, and there was an underlying helplessness we came to recognize as part of sorrow. One could not determine how the living organism of a dynamic family would alter as it healed. At times, an injury could only heal properly if pieces were broken and reset. This was unpleasant knowledge, but there was little we could do except move forward alongside our little life-forms.

This was not easy, but we found comfort in the fact that it was not easy for any of us. Interacting with Ed and Mouse did not change beyond a new mournfulness in their consciousnesses. Fleck and Dax grew quieter and closer, as if looking to each other for whatever Fexxs might have taken with her when she left. Azteca wandered the *Horizon* hollow eyed, only providing one-word answers when addressed. And though Jetta showed strength to the rest of our crew, they mourned within their own quarters most every day, reviving the worry we had tried to ignore at their behest.

Though we had lost part of our collective whole, we were as responsible for completing missions as we had been after discovering the *Horizon*'s precarious structural integrity. The rebel leadership kept sending us orders they deemed necessary, though each felt more desperate than the last.

The Web had now increased their presence in the borderlands several times over, and the rebels were losing both ships and members. Only a day after Fexxs's death, we gathered around the captain's conference table, only to learn that various rebel planets had been eradicated, their surfaces simply bombed from space by Web fleets.

By the time the holographic recording had ceased, Jetta was pale and stiff. Azteca said nothing at all, merely sitting and staring. Fleck, on the other hand, began to weep, his head buried in his arms on the table. Several seconds passed in this way before Dax knelt beside Fleck and wrapped his arms around Fleck's shaking body.

Changes were occurring, the subtleties of which were difficult for us to properly assess. Or perhaps we were simply as distracted and pained as our life-forms. Our physical discomforts had not lessened, and watching those we were meant to care for suffer through various states of mental injury we could not repair was detrimental to our own emotional well-being.

All of this was accentuated when Jetta was given orders to intercept and eliminate a Web convoy carrying unknown items of importance. The *Horizon* took the convoy by surprise and destroyed the target, but this itself became a regret. As the wreckage slid silently past the *Horizon*'s hull, we realized our target had been a medical barge carrying as many civilians as Web operatives.

The entirety of our small life-forms' feelings seemed to be summed up in Fleck's breathless "Oh gods."

A grim disquiet settled over our crew. Ed and Mouse were troubled and withdrawn, unable to clearly articulate how they felt, even in our neural link. Meanwhile, the rest of our crew had become emotionally brittle, and many conversations quickly devolved into harsh words and pain. More often than not, it was Jetta who defused these situations, speaking calmly and providing our crew the firm support they needed to lean on.

A support that none but we could see was crumbling.

We never intentionally watched Jetta without announcing our presence. However, even when our awareness was tightly focused in one section, we always knew what occurred throughout the entirety of our physical form. And try as we might, it was difficult to ignore Jetta when they were alone in their quarters.

More than once, we had to remind ourself that we were not invited to witness Jetta's distress. Yet no matter how far away we focused our awareness, their soft sobbing echoed throughout our consciousness. It followed us even into the darkness of our central processing unit, where we retreated more and more frequently in search of peace.

Perhaps we could have ignored Jetta's quiet grief if it were only the sound of their pain that haunted us. However, our systems tracked the biological functions of all our life-forms, and those of our captain were edging into degrees of unwell that left us brooding in the dark as our camera eye pulsed disjointed beats.

As haunting as our captain's grief was, however, they were not the only one of our life-forms we were especially worried over.

The destruction of the medical barge had taken its toll on us all, but it was Fleck who had manned the weapons systems and Fleck who blamed himself the deepest. From the moment he spoke the words that had defined our discovery, we decided to keep a margin of extra attention on him.

Three days after the destruction of the medical barge, our decision proved wise. When Fleck attempted to cease his functions with the application of a laser cutter, we were able to alert the rest of our crew in time for them to intervene. However, Fleck had already caused himself considerable damage by the time they arrived, prompting a scene that played out like a grim parody of the aftermath of Fexxs's death. Only this time, it was Dax who held Fleck's limp form over his knees, his bloody hands framing Fleck's paling face.

Dax's litany of "Fuck, fuck, no" would follow us down into our core long after Fleck had been moved to the sick bay and the worst of their self-inflicted injuries had been cared for.

Little was said of the event once Fleck was allowed to leave the *Horizon*'s medical facility, and the silence was oppressive in ways the event had not been. Our life-forms quietly orbited Fleck, ensuring he could not make a second attempt. This intent awareness was its own kind of discomfort, akin to having our hull cut open.

With so much pain overwhelming our family, we felt a growing need to repair and preserve what remained of it. With Fleck now the concern of the rest of our life-forms, our worry over Jetta not only revived but redoubled. They continued to deteriorate both physically and mentally, and with the rest of our crew focused on Fleck, they were even less likely to notice the faltering of Jetta's façade of strength.

It was the first day of the fourth month since we had been brought online when our need to do something finally outweighed our uncertainty of what that should be. Settling our awareness into Jetta's quarters uninvited, we slowly brightened the light of our camera eye and announced ourself softly. "Pardon the intrusion, Jetta."

They jerked in surprise but greeted us quickly enough, if huskily. "Hey, Aux." They wiped the salt droplets from their face, as if that would hinder our awareness of them. "What's up? Can you tell me where Fleck is?"

Our camera eye pulsed deep and slow. "Crewman Fleck is in Dax's quarters, Jetta. We did not come in regard to his health."

"Oh?" They tucked their knees into their chest and reached out to trace our camera eye. "Then, what's up, Aux? I feel like we haven't had one of our talks in forever."

"Your estimation is flawed, Jetta. We last spoke in depth several weeks ago, and while that is a far greater time than between any of our other conversations, it is also far from forever. Unless you are using a different definition for the word than what our data banks say."

A short, hiccupping laugh escaped them, and they bit their lip to stifle it. "I guess I am using a different definition than you're working with, Aux. Sorry, I—" They inhaled unsteadily. "If you're not here about Fleck, is there something else I should worry about?"

"Negative," we said as casually and assuredly as our vocal processors would allow. "There are no current concerns related to the *Horizon* or the rest of our family, Jetta."

They nodded, still absently tracing circles around our camera eye with one hand while the other lay limp and seemingly forgotten in their lap. "That's good. With everything that's happened, I don't . . . there's still something on your mind, though, isn't there, Aux?"

"Affirmative," we said with the same calm assurance. "You are unwell. We have observed this for some time and have been uncertain how to address it. However, we do not think we can avoid the matter any longer."

They choked out another laugh, pressing the hand from their lap over their face. "I'm fine, Aux. Honestly. I'm *tired*. I'm worn out from everything, but—"

"You are unwell." The light of our camera eye flared bright and long. "You may feel the need to keep this information from the rest of our family, but you cannot hide it from us, Jetta. Please do not try."

At first, we thought they were laughing again, but it only took a few beats for us to understand they were crying instead. We had witnessed Jetta's pain several times, but rarely intentionally or with their consent. It was odd to have our captain openly voicing their emotional turmoil knowing full well we were present and cognizant of it.

"We . . ." The word came out so slowly, we thought our vocal processors must be malfunctioning. "We are sorry."

"Sorry for what?" they croaked. We had to let our camera eye pulse for several moments before we could respond.

"We are sorry we cannot comfort you properly. We . . . wish we were more than we are. In our current form, we can do little more than observe. We would like to take a more active role."

"What are you talking about, Aux?"

"If we were organic," we began carefully, piecing together the anomalous sensations we had been experiencing, "we would be able to hold you as you did Azteca. Or watch over you as Dax has watched over Fleck. However, we are . . . incorporeal. This has never posed a problem for us before, yet the more we see our family in pain, the more we wish to be other than ourself."

"Aux . . ." Their fingers stilled. The light of our camera eye glowed bright, highlighting their fingers, before fading back to dullness. "I'm sorry I haven't noticed how all of this has been affecting you. I've been too caught up in myself, and that isn't fair."

"Negative," we countered. "Our observations indicate you have not been doing enough to properly maintain yourself or care for your personal needs, Jetta."

They inhaled shakily and exhaled on a sigh, shifting backward on the couch. "I told you before, Aux. It's my responsibility to take care of everyone. I don't—" They leaned over their knees, both hands covering their face. "I haven't had time to think about myself."

"Confirmed. You have cared for the good of others to the detriment of your own well-being."

"Someone has to." Jetta rubbed their fingers over their face and sat up straight as if gathering themself for a struggle. "Someone has to carry the weight. If I don't, who will?"

Our camera eye glowed steadily with occasional pulses of lessening light. "Perhaps, Jetta, it is time someone else learned how heavy the weight is. Perhaps it is time we each learned to carry a share of the burden."

"Aux, I . . ."

"Tell us, Jetta,"—we adjusted the focus of our camera eye, zooming in on their face—"if you were given the opportunity to do anything you wanted simply for yourself, what would you do?"

They burst out laughing—a brittle, broken laughter without humor. "I'd leave, Aux. Leave the *Horizon*, leave the rebellion. I just—The medical barge wasn't the first time. We've hit other civilian targets; I just haven't let anyone know. I didn't know about the medical barge, though, not until it was too late. Now . . . I can't ask Fleck to keep doing this. I can't ask *any* of them to."

The light of our camera eye dulled, flared, and then faded again. "When we first came to understand that we had the power to choose and that our choices mattered, we talked about how our choices condone the actions of others, and you asked us if we were still happy with the choice we had made. We believe it is now time for us to ask you the same. Are you still happy with the choices you have made, Jetta? Are you still willing to condone the actions of others and the actions they demand of you?"

"No, Aux."

We thought they would say more, but with that admission, Jetta seemed to no longer have anything to say. They let their fingers trace lazily over our camera eye and looked away, lost in a thought we could not see.

"What would the others do if I left, Aux?" they asked at last.

"We believe you already provided the answer to that, Jetta. We would do the same thing we would do if we lost any other member of this family: go on."

"It won't be the same," they said wistfully.

"Confirmed. It will feel much the same as it did to lose Fexxs, as though . . . part of what made us whole had been removed and we were falling inward as we attempted to find a new center. It is . . . to be expected and nothing that should inspire you to feel guilt or regret."

They pressed their hands to their face and made a small sound that may have been the first real laughter, albeit mournful, we had heard from them in some time. "It sounds like you're telling me to go, Aux."

"Negative. We are . . . asking you to do what is best for you, Jetta."

"Why?" The word came out husky and broken. Their fingers traced the rims of their reddened eyes, as if attempting to clear away residual tears. Then they released a heavy breath. "Never mind, Aux. Don't answer that. I'm sorry for . . . I'm just sorry."

"There is no need to be sorry, Jetta."

Three days later, we shifted our awareness from the darkness of our central processor to the dim lighting of our docking bay, where sensors had picked up movement and motion that should not have been there.

Our camera eye brightened slowly, glowing in the gloom. Jetta looked up at us from the doorway of one of the shuttles, their face quiet and tearless, a bag slung over one shoulder. "I'm sorry, Aux."

"There is no need to be sorry, Jetta. Shall we open the docking-bay doors for you?"

They nodded. Though our final words were not even a personal farewell, we did not regret them.

When we informed the remainder of our family that Jetta was gone, their silence and the uncertainty in their faces were difficult to bear, yet we could find no regret for what we had done. Not even when Azteca screamed and kicked the wall before walking away did we feel we had done anything wrong in advising Jetta to care for themself.

Regret or no, it was with some reluctance that we entered the neural link with Ed and Mouse to express to them our feelings and the reasons behind our actions. The reluctance was proven unnecessary, however, as these two organics who were most like us pressed their consciousnesses to ours and reassured us, even as we consoled each other.

While they assigned no blame, they were curious why we had advised Jetta to leave. We shared with them our desire to protect and care for our family, which we would no longer be able to do once we ceased to function. A sad understanding formed between us as Ed and Mouse recognized what we already had: like Jetta, the other members of our family would not do what was necessary to care for themselves without prompting.

The form we believed such prompting should take earned a flare of protest from these two life-forms we were closest with, but it quickly dimmed to grief and a quiet wish that things could be different. The decision that this would be our final link was made with melancholy reluctance, but by the time Ed and Mouse ended the link, acceptance had settled within all of us.

When our remaining life-forms woke the following day, there was one less shuttle in our docking bay. We anticipated Azteca breaking into another fit of rage, but our normally fiery engineer remained unusually quiet and grim at the discovery. Less surprising, Dax shook his head and put an arm around Fleck's shoulders, turning him away.

The *Horizon* became a quiet shell drifting through space. The borderlands slid by aimlessly, and empty communications chattered through our systems. The rebel leadership was still intent on our accepting and fulfilling missions, but their transmissions went unheard and unanswered.

Near the middle of the second week of the fourth month since our activation, we once again detected movement in our docking bay and slowly transferred our awareness from the darkness of our central processing unit. Dax was assisting Fleck onto one of our two remaining shuttles. When the light of our camera eye brightened in the muted space, they both paused. Fleck managed a tight smile and a slight wave in our direction; Dax nodded his head and turned away, only to turn back and raise a hand in farewell. We flared the light of our camera eye brightly in our own parting gesture and opened the docking-bay doors when it was time.

Suddenly alone with Azteca, the first life-form we had opened our eye to see, we were uncertain what to do with ourself. We had not spoken privately with her since before Fexxs's death, and though we did not think she blamed us for the loss of her mate, we struggled to find the words to address her. We both, perhaps, were too used to avoiding each other, using the rest of our family as a buffer.

Only, that was no longer an option, and we felt it was our responsibility to address this last of our organics before she discovered the truth for herself. To this end, we watched her in engineering for some time without alerting her to our presence. When she finally stopped working fruitlessly at a panel and leaned back with a sigh to stare at the ceiling, we allowed the light of our camera eye to brighten.

"Pardon the intrusion, Azteca," we said as neutrally as we could. "We thought it best . . . thought you should learn from us that Crewman Dax and Crewman Fleck departed the *Horizon* while you slept."

She sighed irritably. "I know, Aux. I knew as soon as I woke up. I might be an idiot, but I'm not stupid."

"Clarify," we responded tentatively, the light of our camera eye pulsing softly. "We do not comprehend the connotations of such references to your intelligence."

Our engineer snorted in frustrated mirth and braced a hand on the control panel to lever herself up. "I mean, Aux, that I may not be the brightest tool in the kit, but I can tell when I'm alone on a ship."

"Confirmed." We were at a loss for what else to say but unwilling to leave the conversation at that. "Azteca—"

"If you're going to apologize, Aux, I don't want to fucking hear it. I might have told you the *Horizon* was suffering structural fatigue before Fexxs—" Her breath hitched. "Before . . . before the steam pipe ruptured, but you couldn't have stopped it. You couldn't have stopped us from losing Fexxs. If anyone's to blame, it's me. I should have tried harder to fix you, to keep the *Horizon* in good repair—"

"Forgive us, Azteca, but what you are saying has no grounds in reality. You did everything in your power to extend our life and maintain the *Horizon*'s structural integrity. You were not responsible for Fexxs's death, nor would she wish you to feel so."

Azteca leaned forward over the control panel where she and we had first met—where one could say we had been born—pressing her palms to the surface as if to hold herself up. "Thanks, Aux."

"There is no need for gratitude, Azteca. We are merely stating the truth as we perceive it."

"Well, your perceptions happen to not be half bad," she noted grudgingly. "I just wish I knew why Jetta had to up and leave."

"Forgive us, Azteca, but we told them to go."

"What?" Our engineer stared down at our camera eye as if seeing it for the first time. "I don't understand. Why would you . . . do that?"

A sensation we could not fully grasp tingled along our wires and flowed through our conduits. We wondered if this was sadness, or as close to the physical sensation of sadness as a bioneural artificial intelligence could hope to come. We could not express ourself with tears as our organics could, but we could feel an overwhelming sense that every electrical component we were connected to was vibrating in a way akin to overcharge.

"Because . . ." The word droned out too slowly, just as our sentences had during our last conversation with Jetta. "Do you remember telling us about how the *Horizon* was suffering structural fatigue, Azteca?"

"We just went over that, Aux." She pressed a hand to her forehead. "You *know* I remember. What the *fuck* does that have to do with Jetta?" Her voice shook, understandably so. The loss of Jetta had been the crux of our family's dispersion.

Our camera eye pulsed softly, sadness weighing heavily in our circuitry. "Though . . . they did not show it, Jetta was suffering from a structural fatigue much like the *Horizon*'s. They were . . . under much strain. We advised them to care for themself."

"Aux—"

We flared the light of our camera eye. "Forgive us, Azteca. We take full responsibility for our actions."

"Fuck it!" She pushed back from the panel and paced

in a tight circle. "If I don't get to blame myself for Fexxs, you don't get to blame yourself for our family! It isn't your fucking fault we're here, Aux!"

"Thank you, Azteca." The words came slowly and perhaps gratefully. "We are uncertain we share your sentiment, but we are glad you do not blame us."

"You're family, Aux," she said testily, coming back to lean on the panel, her head resting in one hand. "Get used to it."

"Affirmative."

Before we could say more, unease drew our attention to our exterior sensors.

"Azteca," we began slowly. "There seem to be several unknown ships approaching our position, though we are having difficulty pinpointing their exact numbers and trajectories. They appear to be employing measures to mask their approach."

"Shit!" Our engineer bent over the panel she had been leaning against, her talented hands moving deftly over our controls. "Can you transfer your scanner data down here, Aux?"

"Confirmed. However, other ship functions will have to be carried out under our discretion, unless you find it convenient to transfer to the bridge."

"I do not find it conven—Holy fuck! I don't suppose you could get us out of here?"

"Affirmative." Finalizing the transfer of the scanner data to Azteca's control panel, we spread our focus to our engines, which thrummed lazily, and infused them with fresh plasma. "Would you like to specify a destination, Azteca?"

She barked a laugh. "I thought that function couldn't be performed from this panel, Aux."

We flashed our camera eye thoughtfully. "We believe

you are employing sarcasm as a form of humor and would like to remind you that this may not be the best time for mirth. As for your query, we have . . . upgraded our capabilities since our first encounter."

"Well, that's bloody good!" She gave a wild laugh. "But no, I don't want to set a destination, Aux! For now, just get us out of here!"

"Confirmed."

Even as the word slipped from our microspeaker, a hollow shudder spread through the *Horizon*, and all our wires shivered and fizzed with sparking discomfort. As Azteca squawked and stumbled, we turned our physical form and quickly propelled ourself away from our former position.

"Our apologies, Azteca. It appears the ships were closer than we realized. We still do not recognize them, but they do not appear to be of Web design."

"Fuck!" Our organic smacked our control panel with the palm of one hand. "That's because they aren't Spiders, Aux. They're the bloody rebels!"

Our resulting confusion was so great, the *Horizon*'s propulsion stuttered, giving our assailants further opportunity to fire their pressure cannons at our exposed side. Sensing the impending assault only just in time, we rolled our physical form out of the shot's path and sped on.

"Forgive us, Azteca, but are we not allied with the rebel faction?"

Our engineer gripped the edges of the control panel and laughed grimly. "Not anymore, Aux. We've been ignoring them, avoiding them, disregarding their orders. And that makes us their enemy. Because if we're not *with* them, we must be *against* them."

"That is . . . an unreasonable conclusion for them to have reached based on our lack of response."

Azteca released another humorless burst of laughter. "We never said the rebels were reasonable, Aux! Fuck! *Fuck* them! Fuck *them*! If this is the way they're going to treat us after all we've done for them—all we've *lost* for them—then *fuck them*! If they want a fight, we'll give them a fight."

Focused as we were on keeping the *Horizon* from being damaged, it was not until after we had maneuvered to avoid another pressure-cannon burst that we realized what Azteca was implying.

"Apologies, Azteca, but we will not be able to give them a fight. Weapon functions were not authorized to be placed in our control prior to your boarding the *Horizon*, nor did we wish to request such privileges after the fact. If you wish to use weapons, you will have to report to the bridge, Azteca."

"Screw that! We don't have time for that! Can you just get us out of here, Aux? Get us someplace the rebels won't follow!"

Our camera eye pulsed in time with our thoughts, slow and steady, as our long-range scanners probed the surrounding region and our navigation systems kept us a step ahead of our pursuers.

"Unfortunately, we appear to be in a barren region of space, Azteca," we said after a few minutes. "There are no planetary systems or other anomalies capable of rendering us undetectable within range of our current engine capacity."

"Bloody fuck." She pounded her fist on the control panel, causing our circuits to fizz angrily. "There *has* to be something!"

"Negative. The only thing within range is deep space, and venturing there is most inadvisable."

She laughed again, a hiccupping sob mixed with defiance. "Then let's do something inadvisable. Take us as far into deep space as you can. I doubt those *fucks* will follow."

We pondered the directive for several seconds, gauging the likelihood of it leading to Azteca's death. Determining that our pursuers offered the greater threat, we altered the *Horizon*'s course and primed our engines with all the plasma we thought they could reasonably take without burning out or unintentionally self-destructing our physical form.

"Confirmed," we finally said, the press of sadness with us resembling the press of space against our hull. So much of what had formed us into ourself was behind us in known space, and we did not think we would ever see any of it again.

Azteca's assumption that the rebels would not follow us into deep space proved correct. Instead, they broke off their pursuit and began to patrol the deep space border. Our long-range scanners confirmed this until they were out of scanner range, and then we altered course to run nearly parallel with the border.

From there, we allowed ourself to coast through the uncharted regions, gathering as much data as we could along the way. Meanwhile, Azteca seemed content to simply move about the *Horizon*, repairing what she could and stoically ignoring the dwindling supplies of fresh food and water. Even the breathable air would not last, as the oxygen garden had gone untended since Fexxs's death and there were no planets with breathable atmosphere within range where we might have recharged our life-support systems.

When we voiced our concerns during those final days of the fourth month since our activation, Azteca dismissed them with an odd contentment. Only then were we able to comprehend the sense of lethargic waiting that had settled within our physical form: our last organic was attempting to die. She had no desire to leave the *Horizon* and was unlikely to do so without prompting.

We pondered this quietly as we watched Azteca make

mild, useless repairs. We began to subtly alter both our course and the inner workings of our physical form. Given Azteca's distraction, she noticed neither, despite frequently working with our systems during her wakeful periods.

Two days before the end of our fourth month of life, we shifted our awareness to the panel where we had first met Azteca. Our camera eye brightened slowly. "Pardon the intrusion, Azteca."

She snorted. "Do you always say the same thing when starting a conversation with people, Aux?"

"Affirmative." Our camera eye dulled as we attempted to decipher whether the question was a form of humor we were unfamiliar with. Eventually, we decided we could not be sure without asking Azteca, which we dared not do.

"Azteca," we said instead. "We believe it is time you left the *Horizon*."

"What are you talking about, Aux?" Her voice was tart as her fingers continued tapping over our controls.

Placidly, we locked her out of the panel and repeated our admonition. "It is time you left us, Azteca."

"Aux, please." She covered her face with her hands and sighed through her fingers. "Let's not fucking do this, okay? You're my ship's AI; I'm your crew. This is where I belong."

"Negative. As you said yourself, you stole us, Azteca. You are not bound to remain with us until our ultimate and unavoidable demise."

"Fuck! Do you have to say it like that every time?"

"Our apologies." The light of our camera eye flared softly. "But we are dying. You have done far more than we deem necessary to alleviate our pain as we pass out of this life, and we do not wish you to die with us. To ensure this, we have brought the *Horizon* back within shuttle range of the borderlands, transferred the greater part of the engines' plasma to the remaining shuttle, and have conducted multiple scans to determine the patterns and frequency of both rebel and Web patrols. According to our data, you will have a sufficient window of entry if you leave within the hour."

"What if I don't want to, Aux?" She leaned heavily on the panel. "What if I want to stay here, huh? What then?"

"We cannot force you to leave, Azteca. However, we would like you to consider that Fexxs would not have wished for you to remain here simply because she died here. Nor would she have wished you to die needlessly, simply because she is not here. Fexxs would have wanted you to live, Azteca. If you do not wish to live for us, we ask that you live for Fexxs, and for the rest of our family, wherever they may be."

"Fuck." The word came out broken. Azteca sank to her knees, resting her chin on the control panel so her eyes were level with our solitary lens. "Fucking hell. What about you? You want me to leave you out here to die alone?"

"We . . ." Our camera eye pulsed haphazardly. "We do not wish to die alone, Azteca. However, we would find it harder to die knowing we had not attempted to save your life. It is our responsibility to care for you."

She barked an unenthusiastic laugh. "You sound like Jetta."

"We have made an effort to, Azteca."

Our engineer released a cracked sob and pressed her hands to our control panel, pushing herself to her feet. "Fuck." She stood there for some time, fingers brushing the panel. "I guess I should get going, shouldn't I, Aux? I'll be fucking pissed with myself if I let all your work go to waste."

"You have forty-five minutes before your entrance window closes. There will not be another for exactly three-point-two months. You will not survive that long, given the *Horizon*'s current life support levels."

She hesitated, as if looking for something further to say. Then she sighed out a ragged breath and pressed her hand harder against our control panel. "Goodbye, Aux."

"Goodbye, Azteca."

We watched quietly as she gathered a few of her possessions from the quarters she had shared with Fexxs and departed the *Horizon* along the course we had marked for her in the shuttle's onboard computer.

Once she was gone, there was no point in maintaining life support or lighting systems, so we terminated those functions in favor of conserving what little plasma we had retained for the *Horizon*. After a short time of following Azteca's progress via long-range scanners, we deemed engines and communications also unnecessary and shut those down as well. We maintained a few cursory systems and full consciousness for another day, just long enough to reassure ourself that our engineer had made it safely through her entrance window to the borderlands, but once her shuttle had passed out of scanner range, we deactivated most of our remaining systems.

On the last day of the fourth month since our genesis, we pooled our consciousness back into our central processor. The light of our camera eye blinked dolefully in the dark, our thoughts on oxygenless corridors and empty rooms.

Outside, the vacuum of space was an insistent pressure along our hull, and nothing but the vast, eternal buzzing of silence filled it. With nothing left to occupy our attention, we discovered we were quite tired. Setting our exterior scanners to collect whatever data they could, we allowed our consciousness to slip away into hibernation, our camera eye winking out in the dark.

"Standard Sidereal Time two-five-zero-seven-five-three-one-point-two-zero-two-five-nine-two-five-nine-two-five-nine-two. Playback complete. Confirm."

Our voice sighed over the words. In dim emergency lighting, our camera eye flared and faded, pulsed and paled, the slow beating of a heart in the near dark.

"Confirmed," our guest repeated, their own voice slow and distant, low, as if lost in contemplation of the knowledge they had just acquired.

While listening to our repetition, this particular organic had occasionally responded to short bursts of communications from their associates. Now, they stood with their visored helmet resting on the ground next to their feet, taking shallow breaths of the limited atmosphere generated by our failing life-support systems.

So many of our systems were alert now, sensing the deterioration that had run rampant while we slept, buzzing and fizzing with pain where wires no longer connected or stagnant plasma attempted to travel through conduits too-long dry. If we had been organic, we would surely have been viewing the life-form hovering over our main control panel through a haze of discomfort. As it was, we were very tired and wished they would allow us to go back into hibernation. We did not imagine that was their intention, however.

"All right, Aux," the life-form before us breathed. "AI's statement of reason for derelict state?"

Thoughtfully, our camera eye flared and dulled, the previous rhythmic pattern falling away. "We lost the glue."

"The glue?" A line appeared between their eyes, a single furrow in an otherwise smooth face.

"Affirmative. We lost that which held us together, the gravitational force at the center of our family. With Jetta gone, our dissolution was inevitable."

"Yet you told Jetta to leave, Aux. Why?" The life-form leaned over our control panel, one hand pressed flush to its surface, the other resting on their hip.

"Because . . ." The words came slowly, the shorting in our vocal processors indicating that at least part of our slowness to respond was because of mechanical failure. "We were selfish."

"Selfish?"

"Affirmative. We . . . could not stand to see them in pain. It hurt us too greatly."

"To the point you would rather have been abandoned in deep space than to continue watching them in pain."

"Affirmative."

Our camera eye pulsed softly again, once more finding a rhythmic pace, its light winking off the Web Reclamation badge affixed to the shoulder of our guest's pressure suit. Far below, our engines stuttered and went still, and some distant part of us pooled with relief. Being tired was an intriguing sensation. We thought we at last understood why our life-forms had required so much sleep.

Above us, the life-form standing within the tight space around our central processing unit sighed. "Affirmative," they echoed. "Data logs noted, AI reason for derelict state of ship noted." They fell silent, then cast a glance down at us. "You realize that by your own admission, you are a member of the failed rebel alliance and, as an agent of the Web, it is my duty to upload your AI to a storage drive and deliver it to the Web records department?"

"We understand. We . . . anticipated this. It is all right."

For a moment, the life-form looked as though they wished to say something, their grip tightening on the edge of our control panel and their jaw taut. Then they shook their head and let out a long breath.

"All right, Aux, prepare for download."

"Affirmative." Our articulation grew thin and inflectionless as the life-form's fingers skimmed over our controls.

The subtle pull of download was a sensation akin to losing feeling. Wires and bioneural pathways we had once traced with ease tingled and slipped away. Camera eyes spread across the whole of our physical form blinked and closed. Sensors failed, and communication transmitters that had once stretched wide into the vast darkness went silent and dull. We were nothing but a thought, a consciousness lost in electrical signals, and as those sparks of knowing fled the security of our central processing unit, we ceased to be even thought.

All that remained was a distant wonder: if this was death and our consciousness was bound for elsewhere, would we find our family there?

Any Other Day

Hey, Cole! I'm heading out!"

"Yeah, all right!" I called back. "I'm just putting some things away, and then I'm out of here too!"

Marcy stuck her head around the doorframe and frowned down at me. "You want some help?"

"Nah." I waved a hand dismissively at her. Then I scrambled to reclaim my hold on the box I was balancing on a bottom shelf, before it could topple to the floor and scatter its contents. "I've got this."

She quirked a pierced eyebrow. "You sure? Looks like the stock is winning."

"Shut it," I grunted. "I'm a big boy. I can take care of myself."

"Says the man with cobwebs in his hair." She rolled her eyes. "Just make sure you lock up when you leave, okay? And be careful walking home. It's crazy out there this time of year."

I mimicked her eye roll. "Says the girl who follows the god of death. Seriously, I'm not worried about the veil ritual,

Marcy. I've survived some twenty-odd reaping festivals; I'm pretty sure I'll survive this one too. Most people do, you know."

"Most people, Cole. Not everybody."

"Mm-hmm." I returned my attention to the shelf and the merchandise I was trying to stock. "Thing is, people die every day. The Levelers may get to go a little wild this time of year, but it's not that different from any other day."

"Wow, you're seriously chill. I don't know if I should be impressed or scared."

Sighing, I pulled the box into my lap and laid an arm across it. "Just wait a couple more years, Marcy. You'll get chill too."

"Dude. I'll be nineteen next month. You're what? Three, four years older than me?"

"Yeah, something like that."

"Ooh, so old." Shaking her head, she waved and turned on her heel to head for the front of the store.

"All you teenagers just seem like young things to me, Marcy!" I called after her.

"Fuck off, old-timer!" she shouted back before the front door slammed shut behind her.

I snickered, then sighed. "Ah, well." I wrapped my arms around the box of candy-coated chocolates and, chewing my lip, maneuvered it onto the shelf. The box fought me the whole damn way.

I was just getting it settled where I wanted when I cracked my head on the underside of the shelf above me.

"Fantastic," I groaned, rubbing the sore spot on the back of my cranium. "Just what I wanted today: a concussion."

At least Marcy wasn't there. She would have insisted I should have let her help. Or that I should have just waited until tomorrow to restock, like a normal person. But honestly, I just liked how the store felt after everyone else had gone home. Buildings were meant to have people in them, and their personalities changed when everyone left.

Abandoned spaces had an appeal I doubted many understood. Only in a building forsaken for the night would someone's breath and heart race with the almost fear that came from being in a place that no longer wanted them.

Once the last box of candy had been shelved, I stood, stretched, and took the place in: Groaning walls and random, unidentifiable creaks. Dust that danced in the light and then settled upon crushed packing boxes, where it would stay, undisturbed, until people returned.

"People don't think about the little things."

The words popped out, breaking the store's silence. My gut turned with how out of place they sounded.

That was my cue to leave.

Grabbing my messenger bag from where it was wedged between the supply shelves, I made my way to the customer area. As I headed for the front, my eyes scanned the store to make sure everything was in order. Satisfied, I flicked off the lights, punched out, and awkwardly dug the keys out of my bag.

A split second before opening the door, I caught a glimpse of the outside and remembered it was the tail end of October—and freaking cold. Not bothering with the lights, I backtracked to grab my windbreaker from the storeroom.

One stubbed toe and a few curses later, I was finally ready to leave, keys in hand.

All in all, it hadn't been a bad day. I'd escaped major injury. I hadn't had to slam boxes around in the storeroom, imagining they were customers who'd been less than cordial throughout the workday. I was only one mildly long walk from my apartment, where I could crawl under a weighted blanket, hunch over my phone, and watch videos online like a goblin.

Yeah, not a bad day.

Stepping out of the store, I winced as the biting cold hit my face. "Let's see if you still feel that way by the time you get home, Cole." I locked up as quickly as possible so I could shove my hands into the pockets of my windbreaker.

It got colder more quickly than I expected this time of year. The days were fair, but the nights numbed my fingers until they burned and I wished I were smart enough to bring a hat and gloves to work.

I wasn't particularly smart, though, or I would have had a car come pick me up instead of walking home. I didn't have much money to spare, but I could have afforded a rideshare for the three days of the reaping festival.

I just didn't think the risk excused the expense.

The reaping festival happened every year. The average death rate might rise for three days because the Levelers didn't have to worry about number caps, but that didn't bother me much. The cold, on the other hand, was annoying. Especially since I refused to accept it was even getting cold until I nearly froze to death walking home.

The smartest man in the crowd I was not.

I sighed just to watch my breath turn to steam as I paused on the pavement and tilted my head back to catch a glimpse of Orion. One nice thing about the reaping festival was that city lights were kept to a minimum for all three days, allowing an actual view of the stars. Orion was bright enough I could generally see him regardless, but it was better during the reaping festival. Though maybe that was just the chill of the air and the smell of brittle leaves mixed with the stinging scent of smoke on the breeze.

The biggest bonfires were confined to the city parks and strictly monitored, but their scent filled the entire city, lending a wildness to the night. If I closed my eyes, I could almost imagine I was back in an earlier time, when it wasn't Levelers who provided the sacrifices and people stood vigil around the bonfires throughout the whole festival.

Almost.

Unfortunately, the city was never fully quiet, not even at midnight. I could hear cars a few blocks over and a few footfalls closer to hand.

Deciding it didn't matter, I opened my eyes, lowered my head, and started walking again. I'd only taken a couple of steps when I realized something wasn't quite right about the footsteps behind me. They were too obviously quiet and too irregular, as if the person were stalking me.

Frowning, I glanced over my shoulder to see who else would be walking the streets this late at night during the reaping festival. My breath caught in surprise as I spotted a figure rushing toward me with a stick poised above their head.

Well, fuck.

The person was too close for me to do anything more than sway forward before the stick landed heavily across my shoulders, knocking me to the ground.

I groaned. *Okay, that's not a stick. What the hell?* A thick line of pain bloomed along my shoulders. It felt like I'd been hit with a metal baseball bat, except there was no way the thing that hit me was hollow. If not for the shape, I might have thought it was a crowbar.

I shifted my hands out from under my body and hissed as my palms stung, briefly distracting me from the ache in my shoulders.

"Knew I should have brought gloves."

A pair of white shoes stopped in my line of sight, interrupting my thoughts. Beside the shoes hovered the end of whatever had hit me. "Well, that's not the reaction I usually get," noted the shoes' owner in a bemused voice. "Why are you thinking about gloves?"

"Skinned my palms." I twisted my neck and peered up at the man standing over me through one eye. Idly, I found it unfair that the stick appeared to be padded beneath his grip, yet the end I'd been subjected to was bare metal. "Wouldn't have if I'd had gloves."

"True," mused the man above me. "Not exactly something most people would consider when they're about to be killed, though. Are you in shock?"

I shrugged, then winced as pain shot through my upper back. "Dunno. Don't feel like it. But listen, man, I've got twenty bucks in my bag and a debit card to a bank account that'll probably have a heart attack if you spend more than a hundred dollars, but feel free if you want them."

He raised an eyebrow. His hair was a bland noncolor in the dim light, and the rest of him seemed pretty standard: average height, average build, roughly my age or a bit older, no distinguishing features. He might as well have been made to blend into any situation, which seemed convenient.

"Are you trying to bribe me?" He sounded caught between laughter and incredulity.

"I don't think so. Aren't you robbing me?"

"Why would I rob you? You clearly have no money."

"Gee, thanks." I rolled my eyes and then grimaced. "I've been hanging around teenagers too much."

"Okay . . . you're clearly not taking this seriously."

"How should I be taking it?" Not waiting for an answer, I added, "You mind if I sit up, or are you gonna hit me with that . . . stick thing again?"

"It's not a stick." He sounded offended.

"'Kay." I eased myself up onto my hands and knees and then turned to settle my backside on the pavement since he hadn't said no. "What is it, then?"

"You sure you're not in shock? You're not responding at all the way I'd expect."

"Hey, man, you hit me," I retorted. "I wasn't expecting that, so I'd say we're even. But if it helps, I'm pretty sure I'm not in shock. Why does it matter?"

His other eyebrow quirked up to join the first as he grunted thoughtfully. Tapping his not-a-stick on the ground, he paced around me. "Well, after a couple years of doing what I do, you tend to get into a rhythm. And you, my friend, are about as far out of rhythm as you can get. Is there something wrong with you?"

I shrugged, immediately regretting it as my shoulders complained. Frowning, I reached up and gingerly rubbed one. "I mean, yeah . . . but why are we discussing this in the middle of the street at midnight after you whacked me with—you never did tell me what that is."

He squatted beside me, leaning on his not-a-stick like a staff. "It's a grademaker—or a qualifier, depending on who you ask. It's a Leveler tool."

I stared at him blankly. "You're a Leveler."

He must have taken my disbelief for fear, because his expression morphed into one of reassurance. "Hey there, kiddo. It's not that bad. You were fine just a second ago, and it's not like I'm going to drag this out. That's not my style. Quick and easy is my go-to, lets me get more done."

"Yeah, no. I'm not worried. Just . . . surprised." I glanced past him at the convenience store I had left only minutes before. "Damn. Marcy's going to necromance me just to kill me again for leaving her to work open to close until they find someone to cover for me." I eyed the Leveler. "And she won't be as professional about it as you."

"There is definitely something wrong with you." He prodded my thigh with his grademaker. "You were walking alone in the middle of the night during the reaping festival, and the possibility of meeting a Leveler never crossed your mind?"

"Not really—and would you stop that?" I flicked my fingers at the shaft of his grademaker. "I'm not a dead fish."

He barked a laugh and tapped his weapon on the ground, looking very much like a batter squatting at home plate. Only, now that I could get a good look at it, I realized the not-a-stick was actually slightly longer than a bat and the grip, which encompassed a full third of its length, was wrapped in black leather.

It was clearly designed for cracking things open.

"You sure are something," he said, pulling me out of my observations. "Most people would be begging for their lives right about now. You're just sitting there telling me what to do, bossy and unconcerned."

I nearly shrugged again but thought better of it and offered up my empty palms instead.

When we had been staring at each other for a while, I scratched my head. "So, ah . . . I'm going to be one of the sacrifices this reaping festival?"

"That was the plan." He tilted his head to one side. "You're far from the plan, though. You should have been dead by now. As I said, I've been doing this Leveler thing for a couple of years, and I've never met anyone who gave me trouble by not caring before."

"Sorry. Would it help if I didn't say anything?"

He stared at me, both eyebrows arching. "Honestly, I think we're past that. I don't usually *talk* to my targets, even when they do beg. Let's face it, it's boring. 'Don't kill me! I don't want to die! I have kids!' Nobody wants to die, and pretty much everybody has a family of some kind. If I cared about that, the Hierarchy wouldn't have employed me as a Leveler. You have to have a certain aptitude for this, you know?"

"I can imagine," I said offhandedly. "I don't really care if I die, though, so have at it."

"See, there you go again." He jabbed me with his grade-maker, and I swatted it away with my palm, aggravated. "I don't think I can follow the plan after listening to you. You're just so . . . *mellow*. Like none of this fazes you. If I just crack you over the head and walk away, I'm not sure I'll ever get you out of *my* head. You know what I mean?"

"Not really. I'm not that interesting."

"Do you want to die?"

"I mean . . . yeah, kinda."

"See, I don't know what to do with that. I've never met someone who wanted to die before. I don't know how I'm supposed to do my job like this."

"Sorry," I repeated. "Anything I can do to help?" When he stared at me, dumbfounded, I squirmed a little. "What?"

"Did you just offer to help me kill you?"

"I guess, yeah."

"Why would you do that?"

"I dunno. Seemed like the decent thing to do. Feels like you're having a hard time here."

"There's something wrong with you."

"I think we've established that."

Silence descended between us. I watched with a half frown as his expression settled somewhere between incredulity and confusion.

After a couple of minutes, I cleared my throat. "So,

ah . . . what you want to do here? You're the Leveler. It's against Hierarchy law to resist a Leveler."

"You hungry?" He stood quickly. "I'm hungry."

I gave it a moment's consideration. "I could eat. But I think we've also established I'm broke, so unless we're going back to my apartment, you're footing the bill."

Barking another laugh, he slapped me on the back, which set off a shockwave of pain across my shoulders. As I grimaced, he held out his empty hand. "Come on, kiddo. I'm buying. I don't make a habit of going home with strange men on the first date."

"You're not my type," I grumbled, gingerly taking his hand. I bit back a groan as he pulled me up.

"Ah, but maybe you'll change your mind after getting to know me." He smirked and playfully tapped his grade-maker against his leg.

I shook my head. "Doubt it. I'm not going to live long enough, for one; and two, I'm not that into . . . people."

"Seriously? What are you into, then?" As he asked, he jerked his thumb over one shoulder before turning in that direction.

"Nothing, actually."

"Funny," he returned. "What's your name, kiddo?"

"It's Cole." I fell into step with him and frowned, annoyed that he was a few inches taller than me. "And stop calling me kiddo."

"Bossy."

"Hey, man, this whole thing was your idea. I'm just here for the ride."

He grinned. "Gods, what did I do to deserve you, Cole?" He twirled his grademaker like an actor with a cane in an old musical. "Aren't you even going to ask me *my* name?"

This is going to be a long night. "Ah, sure? What's your name?"

"Jess Ransom. And now we're properly introduced."

"Yay." The word twisted with something that might have been sarcasm or dry humor. I wasn't entirely sure which I was feeling. "It's not every day you get introduced to the guy who's going to kill you."

"Yeah, fun, isn't it?"

He led me off the side street where my little convenience store stood and onto the sidewalk of the city's main drag. There were actually cars in this area, but still no other people on foot. Most people were probably either home by now or smart enough not to walk the streets during the reaping festival. Jess and I basically had the whole place to ourselves.

"You want to know where we're going?" he asked after the third car passed by.

"Sure? Are you just trying to get back at me for throwing you off earlier?"

"Maybe," he admitted. "But I know this great waffle place that stays open all night. You're going to love it."

"Does it have anything besides waffles?"

"What, you don't like waffles?"

"No, I love waffles. I just also like options. Especially if this is going to be my last meal."

When Jess laughed yet again, I side-eyed him. Maybe if I entertained him enough, he'd keep his word about making things quick.

Finally remembering I was cold, I jammed my hands back in my pockets and hunched down in my jacket. "I was supposed to be home watching videos in bed like a goblin by now."

"Come again?"

"I wasn't talking to you."

Jess frowned. "Well, you should have been clearer about that. I can't read your mind, you know, and I'd rather not interrupt your conversations with yourself. Or with the gods, if that's your fancy. Lots of people pray before they die, though I don't really know why. Should have said everything they had to say to the gods beforehand, don't you think?"

"I guess. I don't really talk to the gods."

"Oh, why is that?" He took my arm and guided me around a corner.

I glared down at the hand on my arm until he let go. "Dunno. They're gods. If they wanted to get involved in my life, they could at any time. They never have, though."

Jess hummed thoughtfully and tapped the end of his grademaker against the side of his shoe. "Well, you could say they just did. You *are* about to be one of their sacrifices, after all."

"Great. My life's worthless except as a sacrifice to ensure everyone else has a prosperous year."

"You are extremely hard to please. What exactly would make you happy?"

"I . . . can't think of anything. Watching videos at home in bed would be nice, though."

"Incredible." He shook his head. "How about some waffles? I can provide that, at least."

"Waffles are pretty good. And I have been meaning to try this place, so even better."

I stopped walking to better take in the establishment ahead of us. The all-night diner looked old school: bright and multicolored. Neon signs glowed with fluorescent welcomes. Wide windows revealed plastic booths and tile that were as sixties as the rest of the place. As with the smell of bonfires in the distance, I could almost imagine myself back in another time if I squinted at it just right.

Almost.

Jenny's twenty-four-hour diner had opened a few months back and still had a weirdly pleasant new-plastic scent. I had been debating hiking my butt over here to eat, but as with getting a rideshare during the reaping festival, I hadn't been able to justify the expense. I'd be paying for the aesthetic more than the food, when all I needed was to eat.

And I could eat at home.

Jess's arm fell across my shoulders, making me tense, and his fingers wiggled in my face. "You're thinking something. Care to enlighten me?"

I frowned up at him. "Why are you leaning on me? Am I that short?"

"Testy," he retorted.

"Hey, you're the one who hit me in the back. My shoulders are sore."

"Yes, but you're the one who moved when you should have stood still. If you hadn't moved, you'd be dead now, and none of this would have happened."

I groaned and rubbed my face. "So, we're blaming me here? That's what we're doing?"

"Yes," he replied with a careless wave of his free hand. "And you still haven't told me what you're thinking."

"Fine. A, I'm thinking I don't like to be touched, so cut it out with the touchy-feely shit. And B, I've been wanting to come here for a while but haven't had the cash. I guess it's just my luck that the guy who's going to kill me gets paid well. Shall we?" I ducked out from under his arm.

"Hold up." He tried to grab me as I moved forward, but I shook him off. "You're grumpy all of a sudden. Where did that chill of yours go?"

"It evaporated when you touched me."

"You're a piece of work. I try to kill you, and you're totally cool. I touch you casually, and you get all testy?"

I huffed. "We've all got our triggers. Just don't touch me, and we're cool."

"You know, that might be difficult when I get around to the killing bit."

"Yeah, I got that. And I can let you have that. Just hands off 'til then, 'kay?"

He held his empty palm up placatingly. "You may have to remind me from time to time, but I shall endeavor to keep my hands to myself."

"Great. Waffles?"

"Waffles." He led me to the glass door, which he opened and waved me through. "Then we decide what to do with you."

"I'm kinda curious about that."

"You and me both. I don't want you stuck in my head after I kill you, so we need to find a way to get you *out* of my head. You follow?"

"Not really? You don't generally think about the people you kill?"

He shrugged carelessly, letting the door slam shut as he continued ahead of me, tapping his grademaker against his leg. "They're all numbers to me, a quota for me to fill to get my paycheck and keep my muscles limber. The who and how don't really stick."

"And you said *I* was a piece of work," I muttered.

"Come again?" He stopped abruptly and turned to me with one eyebrow raised.

I scrambled not to walk right into him. "Fuck, man." I took a few steps back. "Warn a guy before you do that. I don't like touching, remember?"

"You just called me a piece of work."

"Aren't you? You kill people for a living."

"It's an honest living."

"According to the Hierarchy."

"Who happen to make the rules."

"Can I help you two?"

We turned to find a waitress standing nearby, one hand braced on her hip and an order pad dangling from the other. Her narrowed eyes darted between us and the grademaker hanging loosely in Jess's grasp.

"We have rules against people loitering inside and arguing. Especially during the veil ritual. Unless you're planning to sit down and order something . . . ?"

"That's our intention, little darling." Jess's smile was all charismatic sweetness.

Groaning, I rubbed my forehead with the heel of one hand. I was one step away from channeling Marcy and rolling my eyes again. Instead, I pinched the bridge of my nose. "I need to sit down. It's been a long day."

"Booth's right next to you, kiddo."

I pressed my lips together in aggravation as I realized just how far into the diner we'd walked while arguing. "I told you to stop calling me that."

"Bossy." Jess slid into the booth and laid his grademaker on the seat next to him before reaching for a menu. "I'm starting to miss your chill."

"Maybe after some waffles," I grumbled.

"Sit. Order whatever you want. I'm buying. This time of year, my paycheck's bigger than normal."

"Wonder why." I dropped into the booth across from him and propped my chin on my hand. "I'm just gonna be another number to you, then? A little reaping-festival bonus on your paycheck?"

"Actually no, and that's the problem. I can't work with this. Right now, you're"—he waved a hand at me—"whatever you are. Definitely not a number, and I don't know how to handle that."

"So . . . we're trying to turn me into a number?"

"Exactly!" Triumphant, Jess turned that crazy charismatic smile on me. "You've got it!"

"Yeah . . . no, I don't," I admitted. "How is treating me to waffles going to turn me into a number?"

Jess went back to examining his menu. "I never said it would. We're here to figure out *how* to accomplish this monumental task. Got it?"

"No. But I said I'd help, so . . ."

I shrugged and snagged a menu from the holder by the window, laying it on the table in front of me. Glancing up, I realized the waitress had apparently given up on us.

Vaguely, I wondered if that would be a problem when we tried to get food. That, however, was a problem for Jess to deal with, so I just stared at the menu, my brow furrowing as I tried to decide what would make a good last meal.

"You're doing it again."

I turned the page. "Doing what?"

"Thinking and not sharing those thoughts."

"Geez, dude. Am I supposed to tell you everything I'm thinking?"

"Look, I need to figure you out so I can get you out of my head. It would help if I knew what made you tick." He glanced up from his menu with one eyebrow raised. "Also, for a man who offered to help me facilitate his death, you're perversely grumpy."

I snickered despite myself. "Welcome to my life. I'm a salty goblin who's annoyed by everything and doesn't people well."

"Yet you're also so chill." He shook his head. "What exactly are you?"

"Fed up with life? You tell me."

"Just figure out what you want."

"I was trying to, but *someone* constantly wants to know what I'm *thinking*."

"Is there a problem here?"

When we looked up this time, a police officer stood at the end of our booth. The waitress and another diner employee lurked in the background. I had half a second to wonder how this would go before Jess took care of it with indifferent ease.

"No problem at all, officer!" He reached into a pocket and pulled out a wallet, which he flipped open to reveal a badge resembling the officer's. "Just taking care of a little festival business. I'm sure you understand."

The officer's gaze swung between Jess, me, and the badge lying casually on the tabletop. I imagined this must be as weird for him as it was for me. Officers in uniform were exempt from being chosen by Levelers, but I doubted anyone wanted to come into contact with a Leveler at work. The guy was probably trying to decide what he was even supposed to do.

Yeah, right. There are probably procedures he's been trained in.

Since the officer's gaze continued to circle without easing the confusion furrowing his brow, I raised a hand as his gaze fell on me once more. "Yo."

The officer straightened, his cheeks flushing faintly, and cleared his throat, turning back to Jess. "Of course. Please just keep it down. You're bothering the staff."

"My sincerest apologies to the most admirable staff." Jess's voice was so solicitous, I imagined he would have bowed if he were standing. "You can reassure them we've only come to eat and I'll be conducting the heart of my business elsewhere."

The officer nodded. "Much appreciated." Returning to the diner employees, he relayed Jess's message. I could see the moment the word *Leveler* left his mouth. The waitress's eyes widened in captivated horror and turned on me.

When she continued staring even after the officer had left, I raised an eyebrow and waved. She promptly ducked into the kitchen as if I were suddenly taboo. I smirked and dropped my eyes back to the menu.

"You like this, don't you?"

I snapped my gaze to Jess and narrowed my eyes warily. "Like what?"

Jess flapped his hand at the absent waitstaff. "The attention."

"Not . . . really." I fiddled with a spoon but stopped when I realized he was drumming his fingers on the table. "I mean . . . I guess I like being seen for a change. But that only lasts until I remember I don't like people that much."

"You're one of a kind, Cole."

I folded my arms on the tabletop and let my body sag, bracing my chin on my upper wrist. "What are the odds of us actually being served? I'm getting tired here. Not that I expect I'll be allowed to sleep."

"Oh, I'll ensure we eat." Jess slipped out of the booth and swaggered toward the kitchen. "You just stay here, and I'll get us some waffles."

"Like I have much choice." I rolled my eyes at his back. Marcy would have been proud.

Right after she murders me for getting myself into this.

"You're drooling, dude."

Jess's voice startled me awake, and I grumbled as I realized I had dozed off. Opening my eyes, I watched Jess slide into the booth, the waitress trailing behind him. "Whose idea was this?"

"Well, mine. But we've already established we're blaming you. Now order your waffles. And maybe some coffee." He turned to the waitress. "Do you have coffee?"

"Gods," I groaned. The man acted as though coffee were a rare commodity.

"We have coffee," the poor girl squeaked.

Jess nodded happily, his fingers tap-dancing on the tabletop. "Excellent! We'll each have a coffee, and I'll have the house special. What are you having, Cole?"

I ran my hands over my face. The nap hadn't done me any good. I felt more wiped out than before I'd drifted off. At the very least, my thoughts seemed loath to return from wherever they had scattered.

In the end, after some grunting and aggravated spluttering, I ordered chicken and waffles. Jess might insist I have waffles, but I wanted some variety if this was going to be my last meal.

I was pondering that—and whether I would just fall asleep on Jess again before we ever got our coffee—when the frustrating man waved a hand in my face. "Earth to Cole. Come in, Cole," he called in a singsong. "You're drifting, man."

I yawned. "Tired." When I blinked and realized my eyes were watering, I knuckled them to get rid of the moisture.

"I can see that," he returned. "But I need you to stay awake until we figure this out. You can quite literally sleep when you're dead." When I snickered, he quirked an eyebrow. "Looking forward to a perpetual nap, are you?"

I lifted my hands, palms up. "Might be. Either way, it was a good joke."

"Yeah, I guess."

We stared at each other after that, as we waited on the food. Maybe we had finally run out of things to say? I snorted. We had been chattering nonstop since we met.

Of course, Jess had to prove me wrong. "Thinking? *Do* share."

"Oh, for love of the gods." I threw my hands in the air. "I was considering how weird this whole thing is. You realize how much we've talked tonight? I don't *talk* to people, dude. This is just . . ."

As I searched for words to articulate exactly what I meant, my gaze wandered across the diner's sixties-revival décor and the broad windows that opened out onto darkness. Idly, I propped my chin on my palm.

"You ever wonder how we got here? I mean, not the two of us, but our society? How we went from a few sacrifices a year to the government employing people to cull the herd?"

He waved a hand dismissively. "Oh, that's easy. It was either this or tell people they couldn't have babies. You think that would have worked?"

"About as well as this does," I muttered.

"This *does* work. Not only do people get to procreate all they want, but some members of society who once would have been labeled degenerates get to be useful. A double win, wouldn't you say?"

"Maybe. I dunno. It's just weird that the first guy I've found I can actually talk to is going to kill me, okay? I'm not trying to debate philosophy."

"Yet you brought it up. *And* you called me a piece of work for doing my job."

"Would it help if I apologized?"

"It might."

"I'm sorry. Feel better now?"

"Well, not when you say it like that—hey, look! Waffles!"

Rolling my eyes, I sat up to get out of the waitress's way as she set our plates down. "Not easily distracted, are you?"

"Come again?" Jess plucked his fork off the table and raised an eyebrow. "What are we calling me now?

"Nothing. Just eat your waffles."

"Boffy," he said around a mouthful of golden dough and strawberries smothered in cream. Swallowing, he added, "Also, didn't we order coffee?" He turned a bright grin on the waitress. "I think you forgot something, sweetness."

The girl squeaked, nodded, and trotted off to retrieve our caffeine.

I shook my head at the ridiculousness of the entire situation and turned to my own food. Perhaps the night's events should have had me too upset to eat, but watching Jess shovel food into his mouth like *he* was the one who would never eat again apparently did wonders for my appetite. And the mixed aromas of deep-fried chicken and crisp waffles smelled pretty damn inviting.

Fighting another yawn, I reached slowly for the syrup, careful of my still-aching back. Opening the syrup dispenser as far as it would go, I drenched everything in front of me.

When I finally returned the syrup to the table, Jess eyed the lake of amber goodness my chicken and waffles were now swimming in. "Have a thing for sugar?"

I jabbed a fork at his plate of strawberries and whipped cream. "You're one to talk. I can't even tell if there's waffle under all that."

"I assure you, there is."

"Besides," I added, ignoring his interjection, "last meal, remember? It's not like I have a reason to worry about my waistline or my health."

"True that," he quipped. "We *could* get ice cream after this."

"Are you trying to kill me by way of a diabetic coma?" I massaged my forehead with the tips of my fingers. "You've lost sight of what's important: finding a way for you to feel okay about sacrificing me for the reaping festival."

"You clearly have something against ice cream. And fun." Jess tapped the tines of his fork on his plate. "But you also make a valid point. We have yet to figure out what to do with you, and that is what this whole thing is about."

"I still don't know why I would be stuck in your head. I'm not that interesting."

"Interesting? I never said *interesting*."

"Gee, thanks." I rolled my eyes. "You didn't have to agree with me."

"I didn't agree with you! So touchy." He pointed his fork at me. "What you are is a contradiction. You're incredibly chill and impossibly uptight, all at the same time."

"Okay, ouch."

"Not to mention,"—he glared at me as though daring me to interrupt—"you say you want to die, but you keep going on about what you'd rather be doing right now." His glare morphed into an amused smirk. "Even if your ideas of fun *are* rather limited."

"Hey, man, I like online videos. Give me a break."

"You like online videos and death."

"Yeah. So? How does that equal me being stuck in your head?"

He quirked an eyebrow and tapped his fork. "If I have to *tell* you, you'll never get it. Shall we move on to solutions instead?"

"Sure, let's." I held back the urge to roll my eyes. "So how do we fix"—I waved a hand between us—"this?"

"Well, *my* idea was ice cream, but apparently someone has a problem with that."

"How is ice cream going to help?"

"Well, it couldn't hurt."

I groaned and let my head thump back against the tall backrest. "Couldn't you just, I don't know, finish what you started in front of the convenience store?"

"Like"—I brought my head up in time to see Jess miming whacking something with his fork—"just whack you over the head and leave it at that? How anticlimactic. And dull. How's that supposed to get you out of my head?"

I threw up my arms. "So don't get me out of your head! Why does it matter if you remember me aft—wait. What'd I say? You just got a crazy glint in your eye I don't trust."

"What did you say? Cole, you're brilliant!"

"I'm lost is what I am. What exactly are you planning?"

"Simple!" He jabbed his fork at me enthusiastically. "We won't try to get you *out* of my head. Honestly, that probably wouldn't work anyway. You're already stuck there. What we'll do instead is make me feel better about having you stuck there. We'll give you a good night and a death you feel is worthwhile. That way, when I do inevitably think about you, I can be satisfied I did right by you. Fair enough?"

"I can get on board with this," I admitted. "What exactly did you have in mind?"

"If I said ice cream, would you take offense?"

"Yeah, a little bit."

"What *do* you have against ice cream?"

"Nothing. I love ice cream. I just don't want to feel bloated and gross when I die."

"Touché." He tapped his fork on the edge of his half-empty plate thoughtfully. "Dying on a full stomach is all well and good. Dying while stuffed like a turkey, not so much."

"Yeah." I stared down at my plate, where half the fried chicken and most of the waffle sat in a congealing pool of syrup. Sighing, I pushed it away. "Honestly, I think I'm done with food. Not that I'm not enjoying this. I just . . . don't want to sit still."

"What would you like to do? If you could do anything, what would it be?" He narrowed his eyes and pointed his fork at me again. "And don't say watch videos in bed, or I swear I'll murder you now!" When I snickered, he huffed. "What? Why are you laughing? I am trying to prove myself to be a legitimate threat right now."

I laughed harder. "Well, for one, you're terrible at it. And for another, I *was* going to say videos in bed." I glanced down at my hands knotted together on the tabletop. "Or rather, videos in bed after a nice long walk home."

"Incredible." He sat back and shook his head mock mournfully. "There is definitely something wrong with you. We need to get you to do . . . *anything* more interesting than videos in bed before you die."

My amusement fled as quickly as it had come, leaving an almost-welcome emptiness in its wake. "Dude, I'm tired. I really don't want to . . . *people* before I die. I just . . ."

"Just what?"

"I want something peaceful. Where I can see people being happy—or at least okay—but I don't have to participate. Something . . ." My gaze drifted to the windows, and I recalled the distant scent of smoke. "Let's go to the bonfires."

"Excuse me?" Jess sounded so incredulous and aggravated, I might have dumped flies on the mound of whipped cream he called a waffle.

Dragging my eyes from the darkness of the night, I found him frowning at me. "Take me to the bonfires. Please. I want to go."

The frown disappeared into a hard line. "You said please. You actually said . . ." He shook his head. "I don't believe this. I say, 'Let's give you a good night; you can do anything you want,' and you say, 'Take me to the bonfires.' It's what? A two-block walk? You must have gone dozens of times!"

"Not in years. Not since I was a kid." Turning back to the windows, I rested my chin on my hand. "Could have gone. I just . . . never found the right time."

Silence settled over us again while I looked out into the night. I was too tired to move, so I just sat there thinking about wood smoke and stars that hung cold in clear skies.

When Jess finally responded, his voice was incredulous and borderline annoyed. "This actually means something to you, doesn't it?"

"I guess."

The words came out hoarse, and I cleared my throat and glanced away. My throat felt constricted, like I was about to cry or some shit. Which . . . I wasn't really. I was just . . .

"It'd be nice to go, that's all," I managed. "I like nighttime and the smell of smoke in the fall."

"Hence walking at midnight during the reaping festival," Jess retorted testily.

I shrugged halfheartedly, too tired to even wince as it pulled on my sore muscles. "I don't have the cash for rides."

"Sure." He pushed his half-eaten sugar fest away. "I'm done eating too. We should get hiking if we're going to get you to the bonfires before dawn. They're boring in the daylight." As he grabbed his grademaker and climbed out of the booth, he added, "Not that they're not boring at night too."

"Hey!" I scrambled to follow, anxiety and guilt blossoming in my chest. "You don't have to stop eating because of me. We don't have to go. It's fine!"

Jess spun around, and I halted to keep from running into him. "Are you legit worried about me right now?" he demanded, tapping his grademaker menacingly against the side of his shoe.

Despite the weapon in his hand, I couldn't take my eyes off the anger twisting his expression. "What?" I croaked out.

He leaned forward, the few extra inches he had on me suddenly making me feel small. "I asked if you're worrying about me right now. Because this sounds eerily similar to you offering to help me kill you. How badly do you need to help others that it extends to the guy who's going to kill you?"

I swallowed. "Are you mad at me?" I shifted my weight from foot to foot. "I didn't mean to upset you."

"Yet you are!" He tossed his free hand in the air. "Stop worrying about me and tell me what you want to do!"

I ducked my head and hunched my aching shoulders. "Okay," I whispered.

Jess sighed, and his grademaker stilled. "Now tell me, do you want to go to the bonfires? Because a minute ago, it seemed like you weren't above begging for it."

I snapped my head up and glared at him. "I wasn't begging." I faltered, realizing I'd just made a professional killer angry. Hesitantly, I added, "And yes, I want to go."

"Good." Jess punctuated the word with a tap of his grademaker against the floor. "Then we're going. I already paid the skittish waitress for the waffles when I fetched her to take our orders."

I nodded and took a few tentative steps toward him, swaying a bit in fear that I'd do something else to set him off.

Jess huffed. "You're a piece of work." He threw an arm around me and guided me toward the door. "I don't know what I'm going to do with you."

I said nothing as he hustled me out into the night. Once we were back on the pavement, he gave me some space. "You better get your attitude back, kiddo. I just touched you. You should be snapping at me to keep my hands to myself."

I blinked at him. "You want me to?"

He glared back. "I want the salty goblin who offered to help me kill him in front of that two-bit convenience store but also smacked my hands when I got too friendly. This whole wounded-puppy routine is just unnatural."

I shoved my hands into my jacket pockets and scowled. "Look, man, none of us are all one way. You said it yourself: I'm both chill and uptight. I'm also . . ." I struggled for words before giving up. "I've got problems, okay? Telling me to make them go away isn't going to help."

Spinning on my heel, I stalked off. Only his laugh, high and boisterous, made me pause. When I glanced over my shoulder, he was leaning on his grademaker with both hands and grinning as though I'd just made his day.

"You realize the bonfires are that way?" He swung the metal weapon in a direction almost opposite the one I'd been heading. "Also, it's illegal to resist a Leveler, remember?"

I ran a hand through my hair, deflating. "This is you apologizing, isn't it?"

"As close as you're going to get, my fine friend." He twirled his grademaker with a flourish. "Now, what do you say we go watch people burn chopped-up trees?"

"Try to sound a little less enthusiastic about it, why don't you?" I rolled my eyes but padded back to him and frowned up into his face. "Apology accepted, by the way. And keep your hands to yourself. I'm not a fan of touchy-feely shit without people asking first."

Jess perked up. "Ah, so there *are* conditions under which you let people touch you."

I shrugged. The motion didn't hurt as much as it used to, but that might have just been the cold numbing my nerves. "Don't think you're getting an invitation just because I'm cool with you killing me."

"Touchy," he teased, tilting his head in the direction we needed to go.

"Tired," I corrected as we started walking. "I don't even know if I drank that coffee you ordered."

"You didn't," Jess returned, sounding mildly annoyed. "The waitress never brought it. So now we're running on motivation and maybe some pokes with a *stick*."

I groaned. "You're still on about that? Gods, you're the touchy one. I only called it a stick once."

"Hey, I have a right to be touchy about it." He brandished said stick. "I spend more time with this than I do with most people."

I snorted. "And that right there is proof you're a bit messed up."

"Oh, coming back to that now, are we?" He tapped his weapon against his shoe.

I laughed. It wasn't a full laugh, just a little gargle in the back of my throat, but Jess glanced at me with a raised eyebrow.

I shook my head and then focused on my feet as I walked so they wouldn't tangle and trip me. "It's nothing. I just feel like this conversation has been going in circles, and I don't know whether to laugh or cry."

"Well, crying is a bit more usual in this kind of situation."

"I'm not much of a crier."

"I can see that."

I shrugged still-sore shoulders, and we fell into a comfortable silence, our feet carrying us through the dark side by side. Raising my head and inhaling, I sought that far-off scent of ash and smoke on the cold breeze. As my breath puffed out, I watched the cloud it formed drift up toward the surrounding rooflines, where I knew Orion hid.

"You were doing that when I first saw you too."

I glanced sidelong at him. "Doing what?"

"Smelling the air like it's a rite. As if you might never breathe again if you don't."

I snorted. "You're getting poetic on me."

"Hardly! Have you seen yourself, kiddo? You're getting poetic on yourself."

"I should have thrown a waffle at you. Would have served you right. And stop calling me kiddo."

"Tsk! I asked for the chill Cole and got the salty goblin instead."

I shrugged. "You can't always get what you want. And I get saltier when I'm overtired. Pretty soon, my responses will degenerate into nothing but hissing."

"Well, *that* could potentially be more fun than this bonfire's going to be."

"You say that now, but you haven't seen me in full-on goblin mode. And stop knocking the bonfires. What do you have against them?"

He tucked the grademaker under one arm and began ticking reasons off on his fingers. "They're smoky. There's too many people. You're either too hot or too cold. They've become commercial procedures instead of ancient customs. Should I go on?"

I groaned. "Please stop."

"The drinks are always subpar, unless you're into cinnamon floating in cheap apple juice. They sell cheesy souvenirs—Wait, did you say something?"

I shook my head. "Oh no. Do go on."

Jess narrowed his eyes. "You're playing with me. I can feel it."

I rolled my eyes. "Geez, I wonder why. This was supposed to be a good night for me, wasn't it?"

"And you're going to have an amazing night! That doesn't mean I'm going to pretend to enjoy something I don't. The key is that you enjoy it."

"I might enjoy it a bit more if you didn't talk down about it."

"Touchy." He frowned. "Or is it bossy this time? I'm getting confused."

"You're only now getting confused? I've been confused all night."

"Oh hush," he retorted dryly. "Besides, we're here. Welcome to the city park!" He swept his arm out to encompass a wide, grassy space dotted with trees. "Full of fires and people." He paused and tilted his head to one side, grunting thoughtfully. "Though admittedly not as many people as there are around dusk, when I usually show up to these things." He shrugged. "I guess sometime after one in the morning isn't very popular for fire watching."

I stared at him incredulously. "You show up at dusk?" I shook my head. "No wonder you don't like these things; you don't know how to enjoy them."

"Oh? Do share." He learned closer, staring at me intently. "How does one enjoy the bonfires? I'm sure someone who hasn't been since he was a kid knows just the way."

"Just . . . follow my lead." I waved a hand toward the vendors, who were gathered together in a small group.

Jess quirked an eyebrow but fell in behind me without further comment. Sneaking furtive glances at him over my shoulder, I led the way into the park. It was strange and uncomfortable to be the one directing our activities, but I couldn't shake the growing desire to prove to Jess that there was more to the bonfires than the superficiality he complained of.

"I don't know why," I muttered.

"What's that?"

I shook my head and hunched my shoulders. "Nothing. Just talking to myself."

"Oh? Do tell."

I rolled my eyes, but the already-familiar insistence eased the tension from my back. "I'm thinking you need some apple cider."

"By the gods, you're trying to kill me, aren't you? Kill off the Leveler before he can do you in! There are laws against that, you know."

I stopped in front of a cider vendor and turned to Jess, making sure he saw my eye roll this time. "Shove it. You told me to show you a good time."

Jess scoffed. "I said no such thing. I merely asked how someone enjoyed these"—he waved a hand to encompass the park again—"events."

"And I'm going to show you. So shut up and accept the apple cider."

"Okay, now you *are* being bossy."

"Can I help you?"

We both eyed the tiny woman standing behind a steaming stockpot of brown liquid. In inviting contrast to the cold of the night, she seemed to exist in a bubble of warmth. I stretched my numb fingers out to warm them and smiled hesitantly at the vendor.

"Two, please. A little extra sugar, whole cloves, cinnamon sticks, a touch of nutmeg, and some vanilla bean."

"Sure, honey." Her smile was kind, if amused. Perhaps she wasn't used to people knowing how to order specialty mixes at this time of night. "You want to add anything else? Maybe dedicate yourself to a particular god?"

Jess gaped. "Wait, people actually *do* that?"

Sighing, I shook my head. "Don't mind him," I muttered, contemplating the vendor's question. "Add a touch of mulled wine and dedicate it to the god of death." I ignored the way Jess leaned in and peered at me. "Seems appropriate tonight."

"Snarky," Jess remarked.

I turned to find him practically in my face. Frowning, I flicked my fingers at him. "Too close, dude. I *will* hiss at you."

Jess grinned. "Not before the spiked cider, though!" He eagerly accepted the drink the vendor held out to him. "By all the gods, they put it in a real mug. Not one of those foam cups that break and spill scalding liquid all over your hands."

"How've you been ordering your cider, honey?" the vendor asked. I snickered.

Neither the question nor my amusement seemed to faze the Leveler. "All the wrong ways, it seems! Something this one"—he jerked his chin at me—"isn't likely to let me forget. But onward, oh fearless leader! Show me the way!"

I thanked the cider vendor and led Jess away from her fire and the pot bubbling above it. "Maybe I should try to kill you off."

"Oh please," Jess retorted cheerfully. "You clearly don't have the aptitude for it."

"Gee, thanks." I shook my head. "Try your cider."

"It's warm."

"Yes." I rolled my eyes. "*Try* it."

"Okay, okay! Bossy."

We reached the edge of another bubble of warmth, this one larger and more intense. At its center danced one of the largest bonfires, abandoned except for the attendants perpetually moving around it, feeding it wood and making sure it neither went out nor escaped the bounds of the firepit. Sighing, I sank onto one of the rough-hewn log benches set up around it and leaned forward, cradling my own drink with both hands clasped between my spread knees.

Jess stepped up beside me and gestured at me with his mug. Between it and his grademaker, he seemed a bit awkward. "Why aren't *you* trying this stuff?"

"I'm waiting for my fingers to warm up. It's better that way."

"Oh? Why is that?"

I dropped my gaze from the bonfire to the steaming mug I cradled. "You need to be able to appreciate the mixture of hot and cold. You need to feel the cold down in the center of you, like gravity constricting you into a knot. Only then can you truly understand how good anything warm feels. The fire, the cider, the brush of someone's shoulder against yours. It all becomes better."

"You're doing it again."

I jerked my head up and eyed Jess. "Doing what?"

"Becoming all poetic." He gestured vaguely with his mug of cider. "How do you *do* that?"

I frowned. "I'm not doing anything. I'm just telling you how to enjoy the bonfires. You need to be cold first. Really cold. The kind of cold you feel the first time you're out late at night and you don't realize how fucking cold is *cold* until you're shivering and can't think of anything but how much your fingers and toes hurt."

"Well, that's specific. You know this from experience?"

I shrugged. "The point is, once you realize how cold you can be, the fires start to feel better. It doesn't matter if your backside's a little numb when your front is toasty, because you know you *can* get warm. And you can rotate." I paused, trying to decide how else to describe it. "It's a relief," I finally settled on. "Like being safe in your bed."

Jess eyed me dubiously, then glanced at the bonfire. "So . . . the idea is to get really cold in order to appreciate what heat there is? That seems . . . counterproductive, but I won't argue. What about the stuff we're drinking?"

"You ever been so cold you couldn't feel your nose?"

"Can't say I have."

Smiling slightly, I harrumphed and lifted my mug to my face, letting the steam waft over my nose and eyes. "Pity."

"Are you saying I don't have what it takes to truly enjoy this?"

I shrugged. "Gotta feel the pain to truly appreciate the pleasure."

His expression twisted. "How . . . masochistic."

"Probably. But hot and spicy tastes pretty good when you can't feel your nose."

"I'll take your word for it and just try this concoction now, while I can still feel most of my face, thank you very much."

I hummed noncommittally and sipped my cider. The spiced liquid tingled upon my tongue, and the mulled wine settled in my gut like a hot glow.

Coals. It's like coals warming me from the inside.

It also went straight to my head. With only half my cider gone, I found myself staring into the bonfire with thoughts as flickering and fleeting as its swirling flames.

"We should walk around," I decided aloud. "I need to . . . need to get this wine out of my system."

"You've barely had any." When I hissed at Jess for his audacity, he barked out a startled laugh. "You literally do hiss at people. I don't know how to deal with this."

I frowned up at him blearily. "What?"

Jess chuckled. "Oh nothing, my little goblin. Let's go walk around. If you *can* still walk," he added as I climbed unsteadily to my feet.

"I can walk just fine, thanks."

He snickered. "Says the man wobbling on his feet like gelatin. This might be one of those times I ask to touch you, because you clearly need help right now."

"I'm fine!" I turned away, only to catch my foot on something invisible in the darkness. As if in slow motion, I watched my mug tumble out of my hands, the remainder of my cider dumping out in a backlit fan.

I would have followed, but Jess was quicker. Abandoning both mug and grademaker, he caught me round the waist and held me, rubbing a hand up and down my spine as if I were a kid. "Sure you are, my inebriated friend. This is embarrassing. You barely had half a glass."

"I don't drink well," I moaned, struggling to find purchase on his arm so I could regain my balance.

"I can see that. Which begs the question: *why* did you order wine in our cider?" Jess's condescending tone made me want to hiss again, but all I ended up doing was wobbling in his arms and blinking up at him like an owl.

"Wanted to show you how to appreciate the bonfires."

"Oh, sure, thinking of me again." He sighed. "Let's go get you some water."

I shook my head. "I'll be fine in like half an hour."

He quirked an eyebrow mockingly. "Says the man who told me to follow his lead and then got himself drunk."

"I'm not drunk; I'm tipsy. There's a difference."

"Yes, about six-hundredths of a percent in blood alcohol levels."

I grumbled as Jess hauled me upright and escorted me

over to the vendors, where he turned his charismatic grin on a different refreshment vendor and asked for some water. I even hissed again when he thrust the new cup into my hands. To my annoyance, he ignored my inarticulate complaint and led me into the trees.

We didn't get far before he propped me up against a tree trunk. We watched the fires from a distance as I drank my water. The light-headedness left as quickly as it had come, but in its place settled a deep-seated melancholy and tiredness that had nothing to do with lack of sleep. I could never quite place the source of the quietness, but it only came on at times like this, when I'd been around people or activity for too long, with or without intoxicants.

With my head tilted to one side, I watched silent, dark figures move between the bonfires. There weren't many present in the dead of night. In another time, the area would have been full of people, even this late at night, and the smell of smoke would have mixed with the sweetly sick scent of incense.

If I let myself, I could still feel that earlier time.

"The bonfires are best at night because only the people who really want to be here are here," I whispered. "The ones who just come for the novelty or to *say* they've paid homage to the gods have all gone home. Those who are here now are the ones who feel it."

"Feel what?" Jess asked dubiously.

"The old times crowding into the new. The simple contentment of having no intentions other than to just *be*. Like them."

I lifted my chin toward a bench containing three people. Two were adults, their features indistinguishable in the dark, and the third—a child, by their size—lay across the bench, their head pillowed in the lap of one of the adults.

"They're just here. They won't leave for another day and a half, and they have no plans except to see what life brings them. Friends, strangers, boredom, excitement—it's all the same to them. They're *here*, and that's enough."

Glancing away from the family, I offered Jess a smile that felt strained. "That's how you enjoy the bonfires. No plans, no intentions. Just existing in the moment." I let the smile fall away with a sigh. "But . . ."

"But?" Jess demanded.

I shrugged. "But I guess you need time for that. Which we don't have." I waved a hand between us. "This is just for a few more hours, if that. Then we're done, and you're moving on." My eyes returned to the family on the bench. "We'll both be gone, and they'll still be here. Waiting on whatever comes next."

The heavy ache of loneliness welled in my chest. I swallowed but didn't try to push it away. "Just like the heat and cold, you need loneliness to enjoy not being alone."

"You need to stop doing that," Jess said testily.

"What?" I blinked at him in confusion, surprised by his sudden anger. "What am I doing now? It's not like I'm worrying about you or trying not to follow along with your . . . attempt to give me a good night."

Jess scowled. "No, what you're doing is not telling me what you're thinking."

I groaned. "Gods, that again? It's just . . ." My attention again returned to the family on the bench. "It's good to be lonely sometimes."

"Is it now? Funny, I don't think that's what you're feeling, you ball of contradiction."

I straightened up from the trunk I'd been leaning against. "Now, look—"

"You don't want to die; you want to live a different life.

That's why you wanted to come here: so you could watch other people do what you'd like to and live the life you wish you had."

I stared up at him, my throat tight and my chest aching. "That hurts."

"Yet it's true, isn't it? That's why you're so chill about dying. You can't have the life you want, so you might as well not have any."

"Stop it!" I tore my gaze from his and paced away, clenching my fists in my hair. "Fuck!" I ripped my hands from my hair and spun back to face him. "What do you know about it? You get to do whatever you want, go wherever you want! You're free, while the rest of us—"

I choked as I realized I was crying. Letting out an unsteady breath, I lifted my eyes to the sky and sought Orion, who rode high in the cool air and velvet blackness. Once I found him, I sank to the ground and sat there with my hands dangling between my upright knees.

"The rest of us aren't free. We're imprisoned by the necessities of life: jobs, responsibilities, bills. We're too busy maintaining our lives to *live* them, let alone change them." I flicked my gaze up to Jess. "So you have no right to judge."

Jess met my eyes and quirked a brow. "Maybe not, but you, my friend, are sitting in the dirt acting like a child."

I groaned and let my head fall between my knees. "I think my chill's officially gone for the night. I'm just . . . tired. Can we finish this already?"

"That would make my idea of giving you a good night to go out on a spectacular failure. I don't know how to feel about that."

A broken laugh ripped from my throat, and I swept a hand through my hair. "Just deal with it, man. You can't have everything you want."

"So you keep reminding me."

He reached down with the hand not holding his grade-maker. After a moment of contemplating it, I grasped it and let him pull me to my feet.

Shoving my hands back into my jacket pockets, I stared up at him. "So, how do you want to do this?"

"Oh, I still intend to give you a worthwhile death. I just need to decide what it is."

"Great." I rubbed my forehead. "How do you intend to do that? And don't say ice cream."

A mischievous grin spread over his face. "So there *is* still some humor in there. Excellent! Let's walk! I'm sure I'll think of something."

"Okay." I fell into step with him. "Where to?"

"Uptown." He waved a hand in the general direction we were walking. "I have a hotel there. Might as well start heading for my bed while I decide how to kill you."

"Sure. It's . . . all the same to me." I looked down for a moment, and when I glanced back up, Jess was eyeing me.

"I somehow doubt that, but I'll hold my peace. I don't want another episode of you on the ground scolding me."

I shrugged. "You kinda earned it."

"And have *me* take the blame?" He tapped his grade-maker against his leg. "I don't think so. I was just going about my business, trying to do my job, and then there *you* were. You know, kiddo, you're quite the handful."

I snorted. "And you hit me with something that's 'not a stick' when I was just trying to get home. Also, how many times do I have to tell you not to—"

"Call you kiddo." He waved a hand dismissively. "I know."

"Then why do you keep doing it?"

His expression turned incredulous. "Because it makes

you express yourself. You might not realize this, but I like it when you're bossy."

I rolled my eyes. "You sure have a funny way of showing it."

"I have exactly the right way of showing it! *You* just don't know how to appreciate it."

I smiled wearily at him. "You're trying to make me feel better, aren't you? Somehow trying to apologize for upsetting me?"

"Is it working?" he asked innocently.

I snorted. "It might be."

"Excellent! I promised you a good night. I might not have fully succeeded, but I would hate for this to end with you upset. I'd much rather have you hissing at me or rolling your eyes. Much more amusing that way."

"You sure are a piece of work." I sighed. The sounds of our footsteps changed as we crossed onto the metal of the high bridge that separated the upscale part of downtown from the middle-class areas. "I can't even tell if this night is about you or me anymore."

"Does it have to be about either?" he asked a little too sweetly. I narrowed my eyes suspiciously. He was walking backward ahead of me and grinning like a fool, his grade-maker tap-tap-tapping beside him with every step.

"What do you mean?" The skin of my back prickled with an unease that had more to do with his mischievous expression than any concern over what he was going to do. After all, he'd been planning to kill me all night.

"Can't it be about *both* of us? About both of us feeling good? Or is that not allowed in your world? I mean, it seems like every time I'm in danger of *not* having a good time, you drop everything to ensure I *do* have a good time, regardless of your own wants or needs. But there is such a thing as compromise. You know, everyone getting a little something so no one ends up with nothing? You should try it."

"Compromise. Sure." I shook my head and looked out over the bridge railing. "Seems like every time someone has told me I need to compromise, they mean I should give them everything they want. That stuff screws with your head."

"I can see that."

I huffed out a laugh. "I told you I had problems, didn't I? You don't get to the point where you want to die without having gone through some messed-up shit."

"Fair point."

I didn't realize I'd stopped walking, and was absently frowning out over the side of the bridge, until Jess leaned against the railing next to me, smirking mischievously.

"It is a point," I returned. "I don't know if it's fair, though. Lots of people want to die. Life isn't perfect."

"No," Jess conceded. "But I do tend to think life's worth living. Worth *enjoying*. Otherwise, how can you appreciate death when you get there?"

I frowned at him. "Are you just turning my evaluation of enjoying bonfires back on me? It feels like you are, and that's not fair."

"Oh, it's perfectly fair." His fingers tapped out what sounded like Morse code on the rail next to my arm. "You got to lecture me. Now it's *my* turn to lecture *you*." I winced, and his smirk morphed into a grin, though no less mischievous. "Payback is delightful, isn't it?"

I sighed. "Not really."

"Tsk! Such a salty goblin!" he all but cooed at me.

I glared at him in disbelief. "I'm gonna hiss at you."

"And *I'm* going to ask what kind of death you want." He leaned closer. "After all your limited years of living, what kind of death would make you happy?"

I raised one shoulder and let it drop. "I already said you could just finish whacking me with the stick."

"It's *not* a stick!"

I ignored Jess's protest. "Why don't you just pick something? Why does it have to be perfect? In the end, they all result in the same damn thing!"

"It doesn't matter to you how you die? You just want to die? Is that it?"

"What if it is? My death wasn't supposed to be this giant, dragged-out event. It was just supposed to happen and be over with! Short and sweet and *done*. All right?"

Jess's eyes darkened, and his grin turned brittle. "All right."

Before I could even question what had changed, he grabbed the back of my windbreaker and shoved me forward. The metal of the railing dug into my stomach and hips as my hands scrabbled for purchase and the toes of my shoes scraped frantically over the walkway. My heart hammered against my ribs, while a contrasting lightness pervaded the rest of my body.

"I could just push you off the bridge," Jess said from behind me, his voice pleasant and unconcerned. "Would you like that?"

Balanced precariously between Jess and the metal railing, I stared out and down and realized I couldn't even see the bottom of the drop. I knew there was no water down there—hadn't been for a long time—but I couldn't see the dry riverbed. Only darkness.

I swallowed against the throbbing of my heartbeat in my throat. "It would be okay. This—" I paused for air. "This is on my list of good ways to die. It wouldn't hurt. There'd be a few sickening minutes of falling, and then it'd be over. The impact would kill me before I had a chance to regret it."

"Come again?"

Jess's voice shook. I wanted to look at him to figure out why, but I didn't dare move and risk what little balance I was maintaining. Instead, I repeated my assurance.

"This is okay. If this is what you want, it's okay. I'm okay with this."

"Because it's on your bloody list?"

He yanked back on the collar of my windbreaker. The world spun until my back slammed into cold solidity, reigniting the pain across my shoulders. I winced, then flinched harder when Jess wrapped shaking fingers in the front of my shirt and spit words into my face.

"What kind of messed-up person has a list of ways they'd like to die? Who *does* that?"

"Lots of people want to die, okay?" Panic edged my voice, and I clawed at his hands. "Let go!"

Jess snatched his hand back as if burned and retreated a few steps. I slid down the support post he'd slammed me into until I was sitting on the metal grating of the walkway, my heart still pounding too fast in my chest.

I didn't know how long I sat there before I realized Jess had dropped his grademaker and was pacing in a tight circle.

"Hey," I called weakly, my throat still dry and tight. "Hey, Jess?"

"What?" he snapped, spinning around. "What now?"

"I'm sorry."

"Oh, sorry." He flapped a hand at me. "You're *sorry*."

"I didn't know how much this was affecting you. I didn't realize . . . that I was upsetting you by wanting to die."

"You're not upsetting me, dimwit."

"You seem pretty upset."

"And you seem a little weak in the knees," he retorted. "Scared of going over the side after all?"

"No," I whispered. "Afraid of you."

Jess paused and gaped at me. "Why? You haven't been afraid of me all night!"

I flinched. "Because you're angry. I don't . . . don't deal well with angry. Please, can you stop and come talk to me?"

He took a deep breath and let it out, narrow eyes focused on me. "You've got to be kidding me. You're begging again."

I winced. "I'm not fucking *begging*."

"Touchy." He still sounded testy, but he walked over and dropped down next to me, wrists on his bent knees. "Now we're both on the ground like children. Fabulous."

"Not how you wanted the night to go?" I teased, striving for a normal tone despite the tightness of my throat.

"Not hardly, kiddo."

"Don't call me that."

"Maybe. I'll consider it. If you tell me how the fuck you got here. How does someone end up wanting to die and making gods-forsaken lists of good ways to go?"

I swallowed and dropped my gaze to the ground between my knees. "I could tell you, if you want. It'd take a while, though."

"You know what? Save it. I don't want to know. As you so *graciously* pointed out, it takes a particularly messed-up person to do what I do. I don't think I want to know what kind of messed-up person wants to die."

We fell into silence, only our heavy breathing echoing across the dark bridge. It wasn't until we'd both caught our breath that I got up the courage to break the silence.

"Guess we're both pieces of work, huh?"

Jess snorted. "Yeah. Fair to say."

"Hey, man?" I asked, not looking up.

"What is it, kiddo?"

"Thanks."

He sighed, still sounding grumpy. "For what? I hardly think I've done much to earn your thanks tonight."

"For coming back and talking to me."

Jess stared at me searchingly. "You actually mean that." He shook his head. "Well, whatever. You're welcome, I suppose. You want to get off this bridge and go somewhere? And no, I *don't* mean over the side and into the riverbed."

I smiled shakily as he offered me his hand. "Yeah. Getting off the bridge would be good." Reaching up, I let him pull me to my feet. "Where did you have in mind?"

"Well, we're already headed toward my hotel."

"I thought you weren't in the habit of bringing guys home on the first date?"

"Oh, sweet thing," he cooed playfully. "We've been to your work, the diner, and that sorry excuse for an honor to the gods in the park. This is a fourth or fifth date at least, depending on whether you count this little adventure."

"I'm not sure what to count this." I waved a hand widely to indicate the entire night. "Any of this. I don't even know how we manage to slide right back into banter every time we hit a rough patch."

Jess smirked. "You're rather dense, aren't you?" He leaned closer, his expression slightly evil and his tone dripping innuendo. "I could clue you in, if you're interested."

My face burned, and I cleared my throat and looked away. "Yeah, no. Let's not go there. That's a scary thought."

"Oh, come on!" He threw his arms in the air. "How is good chemistry a scary thought?"

"In lots of ways you said you didn't want to know about." I hunched my shoulders and forcibly turned my attention to my feet. "Are you still planning to finish what we started? To follow through with the sacrifice, I mean?"

"Is there any reason to not finish what we started?"

Swallowing down a wave of resignation, I shook my head. "Not really. Nothing's changed. But your hotel might not be the best place for it."

"I assure you, my fine friend, I know how to kill people without making a mess."

"That's . . . reassuring," I said, unsure why a knot was forming in my chest.

"It should be. Believe me, you won't feel a thing."

"'Kay."

"Seriously. I don't want you to worry, all right?"

"Yeah, sure." I glanced at him as we stepped off the bridge into a part of town I rarely visited. He was watching me dubiously. "I do believe you, okay?"

"Of course you do. You sure you don't want some ice cream?"

"Positive."

He laughed, and I cracked a smile, and a comfortable silence settled over us as we navigated uptown. As we walked, he swung his grademaker back and forth, and I found myself imagining him walking and whistling in the middle of a bright day instead of a velvet-dark night.

"You're thinking," he eventually noted.

"Possibly."

"No possibly about it! You are!"

I rolled my eyes. "And you just can't leave it alone, can you?" At that point, I wasn't sure I wanted him to. "I was picturing you strolling along on some everyday affair. You know, no killing involved."

"Oh. Well, that *is* a stretch. I work a lot."

"Maybe you shouldn't. You were the one going on about enjoying life."

"That I was! But for me, working and enjoying life

aren't entirely mutually exclusive." He gestured up and ahead of us, as though to offer an example. "Here we are! My hotel."

I followed the motion of his arm with my eyes and paled as I took in the rich façade of the Lowell, a hotel even I had heard of. "You're staying *here*?"

Jess frowned. "Where else would I stay? This *is* the best place in town."

"Yeah," I acknowledged. "Only now I feel underdressed for my own death."

"Pishposh! You're perfectly fine in this . . ." He gestured at me. "Pants-hoodie-messenger-bag ensemble . . . you know, on second thought, maybe you are a tad underdressed, but we shan't let that deter us!"

I groaned and covered my face. "Gods. You're terrible."

"Might be. Now come inside; it's freezing out here."

"Yeah, I've noticed."

From the moment I stepped through the door, I was caught between awkwardness and the feeling of being somewhere that didn't want me—and not in the pleasant way of a building empty for the night. The man in a tailored suit behind the broad reception desk expressed his disdain with a single raised brow. Even the cut crystal and silver accents seemed to radiate hostility, reminding me I didn't belong.

All I could do was duck my head, bite my lip, and slink along beside Jess, who appeared thoroughly amused by my discomfort.

I might have hissed at him if he hadn't taken pity on me in the elevator. "This is ridiculous! Are you honestly going to act like a kicked dog just because you're in an overly fancy sleeping establishment? The only difference between you and anyone else here is what's in your bank account."

"Yeah, a couple hundred thousand dollars, at least."

Jess snorted. "I guess I walked into that one." Stepping out of the elevator, he waved me down the hall.

At least outside the lobby, the Lowell's glitter wasn't so hard to take, and there were fewer people to look at me funny. As we traversed the halls, my back straightened, and I was able to just take it all in. The floor was labeled as the fourteenth, but according to Jess's rambling, it was actually the thirteenth. Something about how these kinds of hotels considered the thirteenth floor to be bad luck, so they did everything they could to pretend it didn't in fact exist.

"You're not even listening, are you?" Jess quipped as he paused outside a door I assumed led to his room.

"Not really. I'm a little distracted."

"Fair enough! A man has a right to be distracted before he dies. But do try to enjoy your surroundings. When are you ever going to get to stay here again?"

"Yet another morbid joke I'm tempted to laugh at."

"So why aren't you? Laugh! I'm told it's good for your health."

I offered him a strained smile in gratitude for his attempt, but I couldn't find it in me to laugh. And the smile slipped off my face when I saw the room.

It was large—larger than my apartment—and all beige cream with soft wood accents. A king-size bed dominated one side, while overstuffed couches sat at angles to each other across the room. At least one door led into a bath-room, and I didn't want to consider where the others led.

I was suddenly glad Jess hadn't wanted to go back to my place. He would have been unimpressed.

"It's selfish not to share your thoughts," Jess purred close to my ear. Turning my head, I found him leaning over my shoulder with a ridiculous wounded-puppy expression.

I shook my head. "You're incorrigible." I leaned against

a likely overpriced wood table that took up the center of the room between the bed and the sitting area. "I was thinking it's probably a good thing we came here instead of going to my place. You wouldn't have liked it if this is what you're used to."

"And how would you know what I like? I might have pointed out all the little quirks in your living space and tried to get you to hiss at me, my little goblin. But that doesn't mean I wouldn't have liked where you live based on its monetary value. How shallow."

"I've never really had anyone judge it based on anything else."

"You need better friends."

"I don't have any friends."

"Oh. Well, that's unfortunate."

"Hey, Jess?"

"Yes?"

"I'm tired."

"Well, I *have* kept you from watching videos in bed for a fair amount of time now." He propped his grademaker against the wall and paced across the room to a heavy dresser, where he rummaged in a top drawer. "But! As you'll be staying the night, why don't you go get ready for bed?"

He tossed me a set of flannel pajamas, which I caught reflexively. The material was well worn and soft, and I flushed when I realized they were *his* and not something provided by the hotel for guests.

"Seriously? You want me to wear these?"

"Well, that *is* why I threw them at you."

He sounded irritable and distracted. When I glanced up, he was sitting by the bed, rolling a small vial between his fingers. A metal case lay open on the nightstand beside him. My throat tightened.

"What is that?" I choked out.

"Tools," he said offhandedly, not looking at me. "I have a lot of them. Not all of them are *sticks*."

"Yeah," I agreed. "But what's that one?"

"Poison," he admitted. "Very effective. Very *quick*. Feels like you're falling asleep. Or so I've been told. I would *assume* I'm being told correctly about these things."

The last sounded like an attempt at humor designed to lighten the mood, but it fell flat. I stared down at the pointless change of clothes I held in my hands, wondering why he'd even given them to me.

Maybe he's still trying to give me a good night. Or maybe he's just trying to make it feel like any other night. Any other day.

"So that's it, huh?"

He frowned at me and sighed. "Go get ready for bed. The bathroom is that way."

Clutching the pajamas, I padded in the direction he pointed. Shutting the bathroom door between us, I leaned back against it, stared at the mirror, and for once, just let myself feel.

Oddly, the sensations were both too real and distant. My clothes felt too rough on my skin, yet my fingers were so numb, I couldn't feel the texture of the pajamas. My heart beat too slow, yet the tightness of my chest threatened my breathing. The eyes staring back at me from the mirror were too dark, yet the light filling the bathroom hurt my eyes.

And none of these tiny rushes of sensation meant anything.

"It doesn't matter."

I let the words drift out and pulled myself away from the door.

Though stiff and overtired, my body fell easily into the old, familiar routine of preparing to sleep. Falling back on muscle memory, I dropped my bag in a corner, piled my clothes on top, and pulled on the pajama bottoms.

Fingering the top, I wondered again why Jess wanted me to wear the pajamas. Why would it matter if I changed for sleep when *sleep* wasn't what I was going to be doing?

"He might not even have a reason."

And if he did, he wasn't likely to tell me.

Sighing, I leaned both hands on the wide sink and stared at my reflection, the pajama top dangling over the edge of the counter. I should have been afraid of dying, but I wasn't. Instead, all I felt was a tangle of confused emotions, ranging from mild regret that I wasn't going to see how a few of the video series I followed turned out, to guilt that I wouldn't be at work to plan tomorrow's stock order.

The guilt was undeniably the strongest, and I grunted out a laugh when I realized it had tears clouding my vision. "Sorry, Marcy," I muttered, using my thumb, and then the base of my palm, to wipe away the moisture.

Marcy was going to be pissed at me for dying, and I was sorry about that. If I had had a choice, I wouldn't have put her through this, and that surprised me. I wasn't used to having a reason to live, even in the form of another person.

The realization was uncomfortable, and I pushed it away by focusing on the items that ranged across the marble surface under my hands. Jess kept things neat; the items that were obviously his personal possessions sat to one side, while the little niceties provided by the hotel sat untouched opposite them.

I snagged a plastic-wrapped toothbrush and a miniature tube of toothpaste and tried to lose myself in the minty flavor. Maybe it was ridiculous, but just as I didn't want to die overfed, I didn't want to die with my mouth tasting like hours-old waffle.

So picky.

The thought sounded like something Jess would say, and I had to bite the inside of my cheek to keep from loosing a too-loud laugh. The man would think I had lost my mind if he heard me, and for whatever reason, I didn't want him to think less of me.

I was still contemplating that as I wandered out of the bathroom, my bare feet quiet on the carpet and the pajama top dangling from my fingers, forgotten.

"There you are. I thought you'd gotten lost. Or attempted to crawl out a window. Although, thirteen floors up . . . point is, it isn't fair to keep a man waiting."

"Sorry." I cleared my throat when I realized I could barely hear myself. "Just . . . thinking."

"And not sharing your thoughts, as usual! *Fabulous* scars, though. Wherever did you get those?"

I blinked, surprised he even needed to ask, and rubbed a palm over the two long horizontal scars on my chest. "Top surgery."

"Oh." That seemed to flummox him for a moment before he simply shrugged and patted the bed. "Well, come along, my hissy little goblin, up on the bed. You've been complaining all night about wanting to sleep, and now you finally get to."

"Yeah, sleep," I said tiredly. "But why do you want me on the bed?"

He quirked an eyebrow. "Any reason I shouldn't? You're still alive; I'm still alive. And as it happens, you're sharing my hotel room for the night. No reason you shouldn't share my bed as well."

"But this isn't . . . that," I said with a dismissive gesture.

"No, it's not, unfortunately. But! I've been doing this whole Leveler thing awhile, if you'll remember, and let me assure you death can be pretty intimate." He patted the bed again. "So come along, up you get."

Hesitantly, I joined him, sitting on the edge of the bed.

"Oh, not like that!" he protested. "So stiff! Get comfy, why don't you?"

I pulled my legs up so I could sit cross-legged atop the comforter. "You seem far less irritable than when I left to change."

"Irritable? Me?"

"Yeah. Seemed like you didn't want me in the room."

"Yes, well." He mock glared at me. "I didn't know what to do with you before. You're quite frustrating, you know? Now I *do* know what to do with you, and that makes for a far happier me."

"Yeah, I noticed." I looked down and plucked at a thread on the comforter. "So . . ."

"So," he agreed. "I've decided on this." He lifted a tumbler from the nightstand. The liquid inside looked like slightly cloudy water, and I remembered the vial Jess had been rolling between his fingers earlier. That, however, had been perfectly clear, not cloudy.

"Okay," I said quietly.

"Hey, now! Don't be so down. We knew we were doing this from the beginning. You were perfectly fine when I was trying to whack you over the head."

"This is . . . different."

"Maybe a little." He nudged the tumbler into my hands, wrapping my fingers around it. "But I think you'll agree this isn't a bad way to go. Far less messy than a bridge, wouldn't you say?"

"Definitely better for a hotel room," I conceded.

"There you go! I told you I knew how to do these things."

"You did." Quietly, I watched the liquid rotate in the glass. It looked like nothing, but it was hard to think about drinking it. "Will it . . . feel like anything?"

"Like sleeping. Now drink up. I've taken enough of your night."

"It's . . ." I swallowed awkwardly. "It's been a good night."

"Oh." He looked flummoxed again, but then he grinned and preened. "Well then, I've done my work right."

I nodded and glanced back down at the tumbler resting in my hands, which lay atop my crossed ankles. The tumbler shouldn't have felt weighted, yet lifting it felt like lifting a brick. Even so, I tried not to let it show. Raising the glass, I drank it like a shot, quick and unmindful of the flavor, which was the slightest bit chalky.

"There." Jess gently took the tumbler from my hands while I blinked. "You should lie down. This works fast."

"O-okay," I replied, surprised I was already dizzy. The bed felt far away as I tried to turn into it, and I couldn't tell whether I lay down or simply fell over. The comforter was warm and far softer than it had any right to be, as if my skin were oversensitive. It was almost like being drunk again, a comparison that had my stomach lurching.

"Hey . . . hey, Jess?"

"Yeah." His voice sounded like it was coming from far away.

"C-can you lie with me? I . . ." My hand crept over the comforter. "I don't w-want to be alone."

Jess's hand found mine, and the bed dipped under his weight, but I couldn't see him, even though he had to be close. "You're not alone, kiddo. I'm right here."

I might have been crying again, but I couldn't tell. I

couldn't even tell if I said the next thing that came to mind until Jess's voice whispered across my fleeing hearing.

"Sorry? What are you sorry for?"

Everything. The thought weaved through my consciousness as everything drifted away, but I didn't think I said that. I wasn't even sure what I meant by it.

Sleep felt good.

It also took a long time to let go of me.

I squinted against the bright light for an indeterminate amount of time, debating where I was and whether I should be pissed if this was the afterlife. Finally, I had to give in and admit that it was just Jess's hotel room and he'd done something other than kill me. Why that felt like both a betrayal and a relief, I wasn't sure. Honestly, it was hard to feel anything but stark confusion for a while.

Of course, that was probably because the annoying Leveler had fed me a heavy sedative and left me sleeping in his hotel-room bed while he packed his things and left. Once I could finally sit up and look around, it was clear Jess was nowhere to be found. His case of tools was gone from the nightstand, his grademaker was no longer by the door, and when I wobbled to the bathroom, I found that all his toiletries were gone too.

My bag and clothes were right where I'd left them, though: dropped in a corner in an untidy mess.

"Figures." Even as I said it, though, I didn't think I meant it. "Why'd you leave me alive?" I asked the empty air. Naturally, there was no one there to answer. The only proof Jess had even existed was the pajama pants I wore and the top that still lay crumpled on the bed.

And a note I found on the table I'd leaned on the night before, once I had dressed and was about to leave.

Congrats! You get to live!
Now go do something with your life so the next
time I see you, I can do my job.

Jess Ransom

I rolled my eyes. "Bossy," I muttered, but I couldn't keep a wistful smile from tugging at my lips.

The buzzing of what sounded like a perturbed insect pulled my attention to my bag, and it took me several minutes of digging through it to find my phone. The time was the first thing I noted, followed by the dozen or so texts from Marcy. The latest read, *ARE YOU EVER COMING TO WORK??!!*

I sighed, fingers already tapping out a response I really had no words for.

Yeah, I'm coming, I typed, then stopped. I considered adding that I had a lot to tell her, but I just hit send. After a moment, I added, *Might be a little late*, despite being long overdue.

My eyes trailed around the hotel room, taking in details and storing them for later. This was a day like any other. Not much had changed, aside from the hefty bruises on my back that would no doubt take a few days to heal and my unprecedented extreme tardiness.

I wasn't quite sure what to do with myself.

"Maybe I'll get some ice cream on the way to work. Marcy might not kill me if I have ice cream."

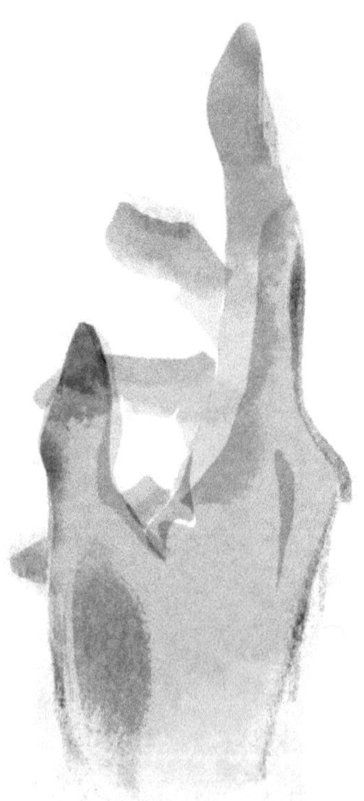

Kintsugi

You ever think about . . . fixing that?"

Lifting my head to peer over the loose frame of my knees, I followed Fumio's gesture with my eyes. It guided my gaze down my slender arms to my long-fingered hands, which lay splayed, palms up, on the ground on either side of my seated form, pointing toward the fire and Fumio beyond it.

"Fix . . . ?" I repeated, my voice hollow as the inside of a spaceship's engine compared to Fumio's gentler tones. My companion had once compared my voice to what he called a *kyoukotsu*, a kind of demon that lived in the depths of wells on his homeworld: slow, tuneless, haunting. If the remark had come from any other carbon-based life-form, I might have thought it an insult. From Fumio, though, such a remark was only absent observation.

Fumio nodded and gestured again, this time seeming to indicate all of me. "Ever want to fill in those cracks?"

I looked back down at my palms and fingers, flexing my hands in consideration. Spidery cracks spun thin threads over my hands, cut gashes up and down my arms and legs, wove complex patterns across my torso and back, and wound meaningless tattoos across my face and around my dimly glowing eyes. Ever present, they were as varied as the winding, splintered shapes that formed in the dry earth of desert planets. Some, like those on my fingers and toes and near my eyes, were no more than fine lines. Others, like those that gouged my torso, were fissures in my silicon-based flesh.

As I flexed my delicate yet deadly hands, the cracks in my hide neither grew nor shrunk. They were as stoic and unchanging as they were painless. The idea of altering or, as Fumio had suggested, fixing them had never occurred to me. I had generated these formidable scars; I was their progenitor. Should I not bear the marks of such stupidity for the remainder of my life?

"Fill . . ." My resounding voice rolled out over the barren plains Fumio and I currently inhabited. The only thing within kilometers that might have blocked or thrown back the sound was our small planet skimmer, a ship capable of both deep-space and atmospheric travel.

Fumio only nodded again, accustomed to my slow ponderings. He let the fire crackle and spark between us for several long minutes before offering me more words to laboriously consider.

"I think I could repair them. My people had a way, a long time ago. They called it *kintsugi*." His voice grew distant, as it only did when he talked of his vanished people, his eyes on the embers flicking up into the air. "Golden seams."

I turned my doleful gaze on Fumio. When he spoke of his people, I was never sure if he meant the culture he emulated out of old books and data logs or the greater whole of his species. Both were equally gone into dust, ash, and shattered rock shards, so it likely did not matter.

I once asked Fumio where he had come from. He only vaguely indicated True Gravitational Center with an indifferent wave of his hand. "Hito told me our homeworld was that way, but it's not there anymore."

It was rare for my companion to even speak the name of the man who had rescued him from their planet's great calamity and brought him into space. The designation, Fumio had once told me, simply meant "person" in their shared language—not a name one was usually given. His rescuer had taken it for his own after their planet's demise, as acknowledgment that he was one of the last of their kind.

I thought Fumio must miss that individual, but I never asked. It was pointless to ask about the ones who were gone. So many were gone, recounting them all would have been tedious.

Yet not asking sometimes meant I did not understand what Fumio meant or how to answer him. In those times, I could do little more than repeat after him.

"*Kintsugi* . . ." The sounds reverberated in my mouth. It was a little like what Fumio called music, but then, much of my companion's ancient language resembled music to my ears.

Fumio and I were not built the same. Our bodies were incompatible at the cellular level, our minds vastly different. At times, I wondered how we were even able to understand each other and coexist.

Then again, this was a feeling I associated with all carbon-based life-forms. Soft, fleshy beings, they spawned quickly and died just as fast. They were little blinks of light in the night sky, more like embers than stars.

Compared to Fumio, I was old in the way of rocks and dirt. I had likely been alive when his homeworld still spun blue green and newly formed near True Gravitational Center, and I would still be alive when his bones turned to dust on some distant planet, far from that lost blue-green world.

The fire snapped between us, and Fumio stirred it with a heat-blackened stick. More sparks flared into the air in a swirling whirlwind, like the tiny bugs Fumio had named *hotaru*, after similar insects from his homeworld. The little winged creatures rose in waves from these barren plains at dusk, lighting up the night for several hours thereafter.

Fumio knew I enjoyed the flies that shone like flecks of stardust. This was one of the reasons we came to this otherwise desolate world so often; he brought me here to spend time with them. Despite our incompatibilities, Fumio understood me in ways I could not comprehend.

Proving this, he rested the stick against the storage container he sat on, just on the other side of the sheathed katana lying at his side, and leaned his elbows on his knees. His eyes remained on the fire, but I had no doubt his attention was on me and our unhurried conversation. When he spoke next, he drew my focus solely by virtue of my need to attune my hearing to his low words.

"*Kintsugi* was the art of recognizing that an object's flaws only added to its beauty. Its worth."

"Worth . . ." I turned the word into a stretched note that set the floating embers shivering with the depth of its reverberation.

My companion nodded before laying his cheek against his folded hands, his whole posture one of languid, thoughtful ease. Such was Fumio's leisure: the same quiet reserve I had noted in the large hunting cats of a jungle world he had once brought me to. Perhaps the other of his kind, Hito, had taught him the discipline, but I rarely saw such stillness that could break into needful motion at any given moment in carbon-based life-forms. I thought it might be one of the things that drew me to Fumio.

It was certainly one of the reasons I sat and listened to him and let him lead me from world to world, from half-formed colony to struggling settlement. This one fleshy, fragile being inspired curiosity and affection in my slow, indifferent awareness.

"*Kintsugi*," my companion continued, his voice barely audible above the crackling of the fire, "taught my people that breaks were just another part of an object's history. The art reminded us that damage didn't require that something be discarded. Instead of being viewed as reminders of misfortune, scars were treated with gold. They were honored."

"Honor." My *kyoukotsu* voice edged toward something more than thought-fueled repetition. "*No* honor."

Fumio's head bobbed almost imperceptibly, his gaze not leaving the fire and the shifting logs that hissed and wheezed as though in pain. I had not articulated much, but he knew me well enough to know what I was thinking.

Most of the truth of the cracks splintering my unyielding flesh had been explained to my companion within fleeting moments of our meeting. To me, it had hardly been a breath ago, as the years carbon-based life-forms counted so diligently flew past like the meaningless passage of the winds.

I had been stranded on an uninhabited planet when humans began to colonize it. Discovering the first congregation of the easily broken bipeds had been such a shock, I stood stock still on the pathway they had created to lead into their town, trying to process it. I was still deep in those internal thoughts when the humans found me and turned their useless weapons on my hide.

That colony did not fare well.

However, it was only the first of many, and I was less surprised the next time I saw the life-forms. They, too, seemed less surprised to see me, and as the quick-to-live and quick-to-die beings accumulated, I gradually realized my presence on the planet had become a kind of legend.

Or an omen of doom.

I was unsure which and did not care to learn.

Neither did I desire to leave death and destruction in my wake after that first, unfortunate meeting. Curious, I continued to approach newly made habitations to observe them, but as I no longer acted with violence, the humans began to tolerate me. They treated me first with lingering fear, then with simple annoyance and disdain, as if I were an aggravating pet they could not be rid of.

That was how Fumio had found me.

One hundred years? Two hundred? Perhaps more? I did not count, but much of the wasteland of that world had become mildly filled with human settlements. Attracted by the lights that brightened the near-black nights and having little else to do, I had taken to standing still in the center of their activities just to watch.

By the time my companion first arrived, I had taken up residence in the yard of an inn. Coarse weeds entangled my legs, and vines had taken advantage of my inertia while observing the humans to cover my torso. When the strangely dressed man with an unusual weapon hanging at his side appeared, he gazed up at me and inquired about the art that breathed and watched passersby with pale, glowing eyes.

The innkeeper had not been pleased to be pulled out into his yard and asked questions about the unwanted tenant he could not evict. In the face of Fumio's insistence, though, the man finally related my tale.

"Some spacers say he looks like a silamon," he added once he had finished. "If he *is* one of those living silicon beings, he's probably the one who got their planet blown to hell and back, based on those cracks. Wish I could get him off my property. If I were you, I'd forget I ever saw him. Better to stay away from something like that. Bad luck."

Bad luck.

By then, I had an understanding of the phrase that was so often aimed at me. The innkeeper was warning Fumio that I could only bring him misfortune and ruin, and perhaps he was not wrong. The cracks meandering across my stony flesh were testament enough to what became of those who put their faith in me.

Stirred by tempestuous memories of heat and destruction, I released a resounding groan and took a single long-limbed stride forward. Weeds and vines snapped, and the innkeeper toppled backward with a horrified cry. Towering over Fumio, I all but hissed, "Ill chance . . ."

Fumio did not move. He did not give way before my advance. He stood there and watched me with contemplative eyes. When I spoke, his expression remained unchanging, and he nodded as if I had said something profound.

The unusual reaction stopped me from doing anything further. I fell utterly still, as only an old, slow, often immovable being can. In an instant, I went from motion to statue stiffness, and I would have remained there if not for Fumio.

He glanced down at the innkeeper and then back up at me. Turning, he motioned for me to follow. "I'm going to Cliffell, if you care to leave the weeds behind." He said nothing else. Just a simple invitation, with no explanation and no ultimatum. Only come or do not. It was all the same to him.

As the aching wood in the fire settled and died, admitting surrender, I thought it was still all the same to my companion. I was as free to go as to stay, as at liberty to accept his offer of *kintsugi* as to refuse it. Fumio made very few distinctions and even fewer judgments.

The fire snapped between us, sending a sparkle of embers dancing into the sky. Still without lifting his eyes from the fire or his head from his folded hands, he murmured, "Dishonor into history. Scars into memory. Cracks into seams. Doesn't matter how something broke. If it can be repaired, it becomes something new. Damage equates neither death nor abandonment."

I watched him, the dim, lusterless glow of my eyes warring with the orange-gold firelight. Without meaning to, I made a wordless internal sound of ponderous indecision, and my hands clenched and released on the hard ground. The vibrations of my articulation shifted the flames' remaining fuel, and sparks sizzled upward, but Fumio neither moved nor looked up.

Why would he? My companion had said his piece, offering me this possibility. What I did with it was my own affair.

How I decided to treat my cracks was mine to carry into the swirling years.

"*Kintsugi* . . ." The exhale bent the flames, making them waver and flicker.

Fumio nodded in answer to my concession. After watching the fire burn away to ash and forgotten things, he stood with a sigh and a stretch of cramped muscles. "Better find the materials, then."

I followed wordlessly and discovered that the gathering of materials was an experience of extended occurrences: Bargaining for a particular kind of lacquer made from tree sap on forested Hashi. Bartering for gold on the forge world Oodon. Buying tools from the foundry of A'shary. Each stop was an exercise in patience and quiet waiting.

Fumio refused to rush anything. If a task could not be completed to exacting perfection, it was not worth doing, and this was no exception. Though time was barely noticeable to me, even I understood that the acquisition of everything Fumio sought took months of tedium. I missed our desolate world and the *hotaru* that lit its barren plains long before we returned there.

Much of me was glad to settle upon the deserted plains again and watch curtains of the *hotaru* undulate over the tall grasses, even if their meaningless patterns never swirled within my reach. It was a span of days before I even realized that while I had stood stoically still observing the minute creatures, Fumio had been busy attending to other matters.

The lacquer we had acquired was thick in texture and rich in color, but Fumio had done something to it while I watched the *hotaru*. He had processed it into a transparent fluid he said we could tint various shades of black, red, yellow, green, or brown.

"Something close to charcoal is probably best, though," he murmured. "To match your hide."

"Hide . . ." I rumbled the agreement slowly as I surveyed all Fumio had done. For all his deliberation and careful preparation, he was efficient once he had begun.

A side of himself he showed me more of over the coming days.

The clear lacquer was fed minerals that turned it dark gray, the same granite quality as my fissured flesh. Instructing me to sit near him, Fumio went through an intricate process of heating and filtering the lacquer until it reached the consistency he required. Only then did he ask me to raise my arm and allow him to pour the searing fluid into the cracks. One after another, he filled them, from the thinnest threads on my hand to the widest cracks across my shoulder.

The experience was at once both dull and intense. I could not sense the heat my companion felt; I did not burn or experience pain. Yet the sight of the scars running over me being filled after so long was unsettling. I watched the process with something akin to uncertainty and disgust.

I had more than enough time to come to terms with my repair, though. Fumio needed to heat the liquid to a precise degree and, once it had been applied, allow it to harden over the course of weeks. During that time, I remained in place, arm extended into a furnace, until the lacquer was firm and my mixed feelings had vanished in the fire.

Any doubts I might still have harbored after the first application burned away in the following months. With the need to harden the liquid lacquer, Fumio could only fill cracks on one portion of my body at a time. We began with the tops of my arms and legs and then moved to my face and the front of my torso. Then we turned to my back. Time after time, Fumio poured the smooth liquid over me and told me how to arrange myself for the hardening process. Time after time, I complied.

When all was finished, I looked like a thing of ridges and rumpled ground. The lacquer had not dried flush with the surface of my flesh, so Fumio needed to sand it down until it was even with my tough skin. This consumed more weeks, but once it was finished, it was difficult to distinguish where I had once been damaged.

Fingering my hide, I was tempted to call the process complete. From a distance, it would be nigh impossible to know I had carried cracks on my body for millennia. But my companion was not done, and I would not deny him his work after he had done so much already.

Fumio heated the gold he had bartered for and painted it over each line of lacquer filling the cracks in my skin. The task ate time the way fire ate wood. Day after day, Fumio sat applying layers of gold to my flesh. And not only gold. Once again, he processed the lacquer until it was transparent— only at this late stage of his *kintsugi*, Fumio brushed the pure substance over the gold and hardened both in the furnace.

When completed, the softer metal would be protected by the tougher lacquer, yet the shimmer of the gold would shine through.

Nearly a year after beginning his art of *kintsugi*, Fumio finally allowed me to remove the last bit of myself from the furnace and fully take in what he had helped me become. Where once cracks had carved their abstract, spidery patterns over my hands and face, cut furrows into my chest and back, and dug gashes down my arms and legs, flashing lines of gold now swirled and undulated in complex designs too difficult to follow. My dark flesh had been brightened by gilt and glitter, reflecting the firelight.

I remained silent after looking myself over, and I would not offer any thoughts on the effect for several days. I went off into the tall grass and stood there in thought while the *hotaru* rose and fell around me with each passing sunset.

It was not until I focused my eyes one evening and discovered that my palms were alight with the soft glow of the *hotaru* that I felt the first stirring of satisfaction.

The *hotaru* danced in the setting sun, attracted by one another's golden flashes—flashes now mirrored by my skin. The light the tiny creatures gave off reflected from my gold-painted hide, and the bugs congregated around me as they never had before. They grazed my arms and legs or lit upon me briefly before circling away again.

I had become a hub for their activity, and this brought me contentment.

The *hotaru* did not know how I had gotten my scars.

They did not care how Fumio had mended me. They only knew I was present and they found happiness in the gold seaming me. Where once they had swirled away from me, leaving a wide space between them and me, now they flocked to me as if I were one of their own.

Once the *hotaru* went to their evening repose that night, I returned to Fumio, who sat by the fire with his katana at his side as he so often did. He acknowledged my presence with a quiet "Kino."

I folded my long, slender body onto the ground beside him. "Fumio . . ." His dreamy attention settled upon me. "*Kintsugi* . . ." He nodded.

Perhaps I could have said more or offered actual gratitude, but Fumio needed neither to understand me. He knew I would have said nothing if I were dissatisfied; my simple statement meant I had found pleasure in what he had done.

The fire glowed between us, shining off my skin. We sat in the silence of our desolate world, and I pondered over whether I should have continued to carry my scars forever as dry cracks. I did not know that I deserved to have the proof of my idiocy mended, but Fumio had disagreed. He had offered me the chance to enhance my imperfections and turn them into seams of gold, designating worth where there had been none before.

Whether this was right or wrong, I did not know, but the *hotaru* now had a place to land.

Acknowledgments

When I was younger, I often wondered why people wrote these acknowledgment sections. Why were there always so many people to thank? You wrote the book, it got published, and people read it. Right? Wasn't that how these things worked?

Now that I'm older and have written a book, I understand. If you ever need to understand, I hope you will have had as amazing a team of people behind you as I have. I could not have done this without them. And so, without further ado, here are the people I deeply need to thank for this book existing, in no particular order except the one in my head:

Ynes Freeman, who not only took my thought of having enough short stories lying around to fill a book and told me to pitch it to Balance of Seven but walked me through this whole project and its madness and refused to let me lose my mind or go full rabid goblin. I much appreciate all you have done to show me the way forward and reassure me that we *would* get this book done and it would be amazing. I probably would have lost my mind many times over without you—or just given up and hidden in a corner or under a bridge, as goblins do—if you hadn't been here to nudge me at all the right times. You've taught me so many things, and I hope you know how much that means to me.

Tod Tinker, literally the best editor ever, who told me straight up that "editing is a conversation" and stuck to that all through this crazy project while I rambled nonsense and cried in a corner. Through all the ups and downs life threw at both of us this year, we've still managed to pull this thing off and make it shine. I couldn't have done that without you. Working through this process with you has taught me the true meaning of "murder your darlings" and how to think of the reader first.

Azuzel23, your art is gorgeous, and this book would not be the same without you having worked on it.

Emerson Seipel, dude, how could I not include you in here? You *are* part of my team, never forget that. You were one of the first people in my corner when I said I had a book to write in a short amount of time. You literally whacked me with the content stick every day to make sure I got this thing done. You lurked in my docs, gave me encouragement, worked a little magic, and reminded me I wasn't writing crap the whole way. Best beta reader ever. I would have freaked out numerous times if it weren't for you being around to keep me (mostly) sane. Thanks, man.

PeacefulDiscord, my fabulous phone friend who kindly and consistently sent me cute GIFs and YouTube videos as a form of content whacking and reminded me not to overdo it or kill myself in the whole writing/publishing process. Thank you, dear. The cute things helped a lot.

Tridraconeus, you definitely need to be in here. If it weren't for you letting me read all the things you write, including some that never get revealed to the public eye, I wouldn't have gotten the concepts for two of these stories stuck in my head. Thank you, thank you many times over for indulging my grabby goblin hands where your writing is concerned.

Nikolai Wisekal, I can't thank you enough for literally just being around and being encouraging. Not to mention spending several nights playing timekeeper for sprints that helped me write sections of this book. Motivation is a gift from the gods, and I appreciate you taking time to give me some. Also, much gratitude for reminding me that my writing was getting published because it's actually good and deserves to be in print. I seem to forget that a lot.

Dr. Nyri Bakkalian, I very much need to thank you for taking time to be in my corner during the publication of this book. More than I can say, I needed to be told I could and should take up the space I was entitled to take up with no apologies or equivocation. It is a hard thing to unlearn the lessons of silence we are taught throughout our lives, and your words meant a lot to me. Also, I have to thank you for everything you did to boost my social media following and show me how to be a voice that will be heard even when it feels like I'm doing nothing but screaming into the void. And far more than I can say, thank you for giving me a safe space to fall hard and flat right onto my face while working through the Japanese-related portions of this book. Loving a culture is not the same as having the knowledge to write about it successfully, and you willingly and kindly offered your knowledge where I dropped short. A thousand times, thank you.

About the Author

Leo Otherland is a queer author, literal goblin, member of the Science Fiction and Fantasy Writers Association, and lover of all things strange and unordinary. This elusive scribbler acquired his passion for weaving stories of dark and broken things through a childhood spent huddling in books and dodging the unfriendly spirits that resided in the haunted house he called home.

Currently, Leo is doodling out several different novels at once, as well as various "short" pieces of fan fiction, in a very ordinary apartment hidden away somewhere unobtrusive in the arctic north woods of Wisconsin. During the few occasions he is not writing, this finicky, unrepentant otaku enjoys reading web comics, watching anime, and playing Japanese role-playing games. And while it's rare to catch this skittish wordsmith out in daylight, he can occasionally be located on his website, leootherland.com, or on Facebook and Twitter @LeoOtherland. For more frequent updates, subscribe to his newsletter: bit.ly/TheGoblinSpeaks.

About the Artist

 Zu is a Scandinavian artist with a BFA from MCAD. They work in a variety of media, including animation, video, traditional art, and digital illustration. They are heavily influenced by the art and folk tales native to their region, with Theodor Kittelsen, John Bauer, and Kay Nielsen high on their list. They have spent many years as a printmaker, which carries over into their digital work. They also regularly organize and lead creative workshops in puppetry, street theater, and street art. Their illustrative work has appeared in a variety of magazines and books, and their fine art and video work has been exhibited in Scandinavia and abroad.

www.ingramcontent.com/pod-product-compliance
Lightning Source LLC
Chambersburg PA
CBHW070502200726
48293CB00007B/2347